Diversion Books
A Division of Diversion Publishing Corp.
443 Park Avenue South, Suite 1008
New York, New York 10016
www.DiversionBooks.com

For more information, email info@diversionbooks.com

First Diversion Books edition May 2015.
Print ISBN: 978-1-62681-893-4
eBook ISBN: 978-1-62681-781-4

Written
IN THE
Stars

SHERRILL BODINE
AND
PATRICIA ROSEMOOR

DIVERSIONBOOKS

Also by Sherrill Bodine

A Soldier's Heart
My Lord's Lady
Scandal's Child
The Christmas Ball
The Duke's Deceit
The Rake's Redemption

Also by Patricia Rosemoor

Dangerous
SKIN
The Silent Sea
Crimson Duet
Haunted

The McKenna Legacy Trilogy
See Me in Your Dreams
Tell Me No Lies
Touch Me in the Dark

Quid Pro Quo Trilogy
Pushed To the Limit
Squaring Accounts
No Holds Barred

Dangerous Male Duo
Drop Dead Gorgeous
Lucky Devil

Thanks to our wonderful critique group—Laurie DeMarino, Cheryl Jefferson, Jude Mandell, and Rosemary Paulas for their endless support and encouragement.

Prologue

Crescent Key, Florida—Present Day

He walked the shore of Crescent Key by the light of a waning moon, his night-clever eyes scanning the foam-whipped sand for telltale *reales*.

The air thickened with the threat of rain and the briny scent that had been part of his life as far as memory served. He'd walked the beaches at night nearly as long. Always in search of a dream. In search of treasure that remained elusive. A legend that wouldn't die.

This was it, his time. He sensed it. This expedition would pay out, give him everything his parents had wanted and had never found. They'd instilled desire for the hunt in him. This time, he would find sunken treasure that would make them all rich.

A breeze picked up—a soft wail that sent the flesh crawling along his neck and down his spine. A warning. But of what? He glanced around. Alone.

And the water that sluiced his bare feet remained deserted.

About to give up, he spotted a large craft bobbing out on the horizon. For a moment, he imagined it to be a ghost ship. But blink as he would, the apparition didn't disappear. A single-masted yacht. *Tourists? Or other treasure hunters?* he wondered, noting a flicker from a cabin window, as if the moon had struck a shiny surface. As quickly as it caught him, the flash of bright was gone. Still, he felt watched as he started to turn away.

Silver glimmered through the sea foam that lashed the beach...He dived for the object before the ghostly hand of a shipwreck victim could pull the coin back to the greedy sea. *Success.*

He hunkered down, heels dug deep in the wet sand, and examined his treasure. No coin, but something of far more value.

His pulse raced...his mouth dried...His breath caught deep within his chest as certainty filled him.

He turned his razor-sharp gaze back toward the horizon, as if he could part the waters that shrouded the mother lode of the *Celestine*, abandoned to the ocean's floor four centuries earlier. Not yet—only that lone ship bobbing—but he felt time dissolve, discovery imminent.

For didn't he hold the proof in hand?

Moonlight silvered the splash of stars tumbling between his fingers as he traced the edges and angles of the ring and imagined a curious warmth, imagined that it was somehow able to expose what he so desperately sought.

It slipped on his ring finger easily—a perfect fit.

Warmth generated from the ring around his finger and then ran up his arm. He flushed and his head went light, and for a moment, he was no longer on a sandy beach but in a forest glade, a clear pool at its center.

As quickly as the image had formed in his mind, it was gone.

Peering through her telescope out her porthole, Cordelia Ward watched the man rise, pocket something, and turn away. She intently concentrated on him, couldn't tear her eyes from his silhouette until it blended with the shadows.

Then other things came into focus for her. The moon a waning crescent, surrounded by myriad stars. All were reflected in the ocean, so calm tonight. The heavens were special to her as they were to all sailors who relied on nature's map. But there was something special about *this* sky. About *this* moon. *These* stars. *This* night.

The night before the hunt began.

Cordelia was already imagining the find that would make her career as a marine archeologist, validate her late father's research, and give her grieving mother motivation to live life fully once more.

With barely a breath, Cordelia blinked, stared hard at the celestial pattern—unusual and yet so familiar to her—then moved to the other side of the cabin, where she fetched her treasure chest. She held it next to the porthole and gasped. The stars in the sky traced the exact pattern on the face of the box.

Her wrist began to tingle.

She rubbed the star-shaped birthmark there, as if that would stop the sensation, sank onto her bunk, emptied her treasures next to her, then slipped the ring from her right hand. Something about *this* night, she thought again, before matching the single raised crescent moon to the first of several slots.

She gave it half a clockwise twist.

The chest, forged of metal, was a clever piece of workmanship handed down through generations of women in her family, along with the legendary Posey ring that made half of a whole, the man's half having been lost for as long as the rest of the sunken treasure. As far as she knew, no one had ever breached the casket's secret. Not even her. And it wasn't for a lack of trying.

She fitted the crescent to a second slot and turned it fully counterclockwise.

On the surface, the lidded box held family keepsakes. But it had always seemed deeper than the interior at first appeared, and she'd come to the conclusion that the bottom was false. Within the design of stars and moons decorating the treasure chest's outer surface lay the path to its heart, she was certain.

A third slot. A full turn.

She'd recognized the ring as key years ago, yet every effort to find the right combination of twists and turns had thwarted her. She'd long ago given up. But now, at a significant crossroads in her life—hopefully she was at the brink of the find of a lifetime—Cordelia let sheer instinct guide her.

Slot number four. Another full turn.

What could be hidden within the chest? she wondered. A map, perhaps? A guide to the sunken treasure her parents had sought for so many years? If only her father had lived long enough to see his dream come true.

The fifth slot. A counter turn.

Her wrist tingled once more. Hand shaking, she matched the crescent to the sixth and final slot. Her mouth was dry, and she couldn't seem to breathe. This was it, then. As she was about to turn the ring, the tingle turned to a fierce burn. Hesitating, she looked down at the angry red birthmark.

An omen...

Then she did it. Turned the ring halfway in the *opposite* direction.

A soft *nick* and the velvet-clad inside of the box popped open. Her breath caught as she investigated. No map here, but a bound book, its leather cover embossed with stars and moons. Inside, there were pages of highly stylized writing on age-fragile parchment. Cordelia scanned the top page and realized it was a woman's personal journal written four centuries before.

Not knowing why her heart thundered so, she began to read.

Part I: England
Dunham Castle, 1601

On this day I shall begin a journey inevitable from the moment I was born on Midsummer Eve, Witches' Night. My nursemaid, Cybil, proclaimed that I am marked as a child of magic.

Yet I am not a witch, for the face of my beloved and what awaits me at journey's end is shrouded from me by the veil of time. I know only that with him I shall scale peaks higher than my spirit could ever strive to reach alone, and because of him, I shall descend into valleys which will try my soul.

My old nursemaid warned me of danger should my choices not be wise as she coiled around my hips the celestial girdle spun of gold into mesh studded with rubies, pearls, emeralds, sapphires, and delicate chains of diamond stars hung by jeweled, golden crescents of the waxing moon. Hidden within its chains is a tiny dagger. It is said the old pagan gods forged this girdle to protect the Wharton women from all evil. I tremble at what may lie before me, but I dare not turn away from this destiny, for it is set firmly in my stars.

To have remained safe in the loving haven of Wharton Keep in my gentle father's domain would have denied me my future and that of you who come after me. I can only record my journey here, so that you may know me and the path I take for you.

I hear the tower bell toll.

It is time.

Chapter One

The beat of her heart echoing the tolling bell, Lady Elizabeth York stood outside the thick, dark oak doors of the great hall of Dunham Castle.

The bell ceased, and she caught her breath, watching the heavy doors swing slowly open.

Knowing that within moments she would confront her destiny, fulfilling her duty as her father's only child, she lifted her chin. The blood of good Queen Bess flowed in her veins. There was naught Elizabeth would not do for her lineage.

Looking forward, proud she would forge the alliance between two powerful families to make them both safer and stronger by marrying the duke's heir, she walked beneath the barrel vaulting, past the tapestries and the carving which made the great hall famous throughout the land. She halted before the dais crowned with the Lennox coat of arms. Framed within the rich purple draping sat the duke and his duchess with one man standing at either side. Both men were broad-shouldered, their doublets braided in silver.

Sunlight slanted in through the high windows, bathing them all in a bright, shimmering light.

Blinded for an instant, Elizabeth blinked several times, before her eyes found and lingered on the man standing beside the duchess. He had the duke's same wide, watchful, cornflower-blue eyes and mane of golden hair.

Her gaze melded with his, and she couldn't look away from the light flickering through his eyes like sunshine playing upon the sea on a perfect day at Wharton Keep. The strong bones of his face knitted together in an arrangement which took away her breath. So deep was the rush of hot, strong longing that she felt tears burn behind her lids.

I need not have feared my old nurse's warning. With a look, my heart is his.

Content and now eagerly awaiting her destiny, she knelt before the duke and his son.

A heartbeat later she felt a strong hand take hers.

With joy she looked up.

Shock turned her icy cold, the trembling rising up from deep inside her as her gaze met the dark, heavy-lidded eyes of the other man with the same golden hair as the duke.

He glanced away to stare at the star-shaped birthmark on her right wrist and smiled.

"Ah, Lady Elizabeth, you are as bewitching as foretold." Urging her to rise, he turned them both to the duke. "We have chosen well, Father."

The world spun around her, as if it had been hurled through time and space. Had those moments of looking into the stranger's eyes and seeing all she had ever hoped to find in a man been a dream she was now cruelly waking from?

Conquering every feeling of confusion and aching disappointment, she firmly clasped the hand of her betrothed, Carlyle, Earl of Seymour, heir to the Duke of Lennox, and allowed him to lead her forward.

His mouth curling deep at the corners, the duke inclined his head. "You are welcome to Dunham Castle, Lady Elizabeth."

His duchess, as fair as Elizabeth was dark and nearly as young, leapt to her feet. "I am Laurel, and I know we shall be great friends."

Surprising Elizabeth with her kindness, Laurel engulfed her in a tight, warm embrace. "You are as beautiful as rumored, Elizabeth. Is she not, Will?"

Her laughter as light as the patches of sun on the cold stone floor, Laurel twirled back to urge forward the man behind her. The man Elizabeth had believed to be her destiny.

His slow smile mirrored the duke's as did the indulgence in his eyes as he gazed at Laurel. "Yes, Lady Elizabeth's beauty cannot be doubted. Much like her fatigue from her four-day journey to us."

"How thoughtless I am! And, as always, how considerate you are, our brave Captain of the Guard, Will Grey." Her brown eyes wide, Laurel clasped Elizabeth's cool hand between her warm palms. "Take Elizabeth's other hand, Will. We shall all be family."

Will Grey is family, yet not the elder son who I must marry? This is wrong! I should not be promised to Carlyle but to Will! I know it!

As if he felt her confusion and fear, Will hesitated before clasping her fingers loosely within his.

The birthmark on her wrist tingled and burned. The

power which lit up the heavens during a storm shot between them, blistering through her blood. She knew from the stark widening of his eyes and firm line of his long mouth that he had felt the shock, too. She bit her lip, stopping the words choking her throat. She knew it was her duty to stay silent in this time and place.

"Am I not family, dear Laurel?" Carlyle drawled, strolling toward them.

Laurel's lips quivered. "Of course. Come join us, Carlyle."

"We all do your bidding." Carlyle bowed and Will stepped away, allowing the duke's son to clasp her hand.

What had once been alive with warmth now felt strangely numb, and where before her blood had run hot, it now cooled, the chill seeping into her bones as it did when she was fearful.

"Now all is as it should be," Carlyle proclaimed in a loud voice.

Agony stark on her pale face, Laurel nodded before a spasm of coughing doubled her over. Alarmed, knowing from what Cybil had taught her that such a cough could cause sickness unto death, Elizabeth pulled free from Carlyle. Honed instinct urged her to help Laurel back into her chair. Will Grey was there before her, and both of them took Laurel's slight weight into their arms to ease her down upon her cushioned throne. Elizabeth's breasts brushed against Will's arm and again the hot, tingling connection blistered between them, impossible to ignore or forget.

They both glanced away, yet she saw her confusion mirrored in his eyes.

Trembling, she knew this is what her nurse had foreseen.

Will is my choice, and it cannot be.

"Laurel, you must rest." His face anguished, the duke hovered over his wife, who shook her head, her fair hair whipping against her pale cheeks.

From behind the curtain, an older man with snowy hair as thick as sable and a neat, short, white beard strolled to her side. The calmness in his eyes, his gentle manner as he touched Laurel's forehead, and the practiced way his fingers rested on the pulse beating in her throat cast a net which soothed them all.

"Laurel, I know you wish to stay and visit with Lady Elizabeth." He smiled. "Perhaps tomorrow would be better for both of you."

Her face scarlet from coughing, Laurel took a long, ragged breath, her eyes watery but slowly clearing of worry. "Yes. Elizabeth, you will find our Charles Grey is the finest physician in the land and right in all things." Both her voice and smile were gentle. "On the morrow please join me in my chambers. We have much to learn of one another."

"I look forward to the morrow, your grace." Dismissed, Elizabeth could do naught but bow. Every instinct, every new desire, screamed for her to stay, to find answers to the questions beating through her mind and heart.

Knowing she must, she tried to walk proudly, tried to hold her head high as she swept from the great hall. Weakened by confusion, she felt eyes following her and knew it was Will Grey's gaze that warmed her body

And Will himself who consumed her thoughts.

• • •

Will watched Elizabeth walk from the room, her heavy ebony hair half falling from the twist studded with pearls she wore low on her long neck. Such a desire to follow her filled him, he stepped off the dais.

"Will." His grandfather's firm voice stopped him.

Looking around, he saw Laurel reaching out one trembling hand toward him, while the other clutched the duke's arm.

She smiled up at Will's grandfather. "Our fine physician demands I rest today before the festivities on the morrow." She laid her cheek against the duke's shoulder. "As does my lord. Please, Will, come visit with me awhile."

Ignoring Carlyle's smirk and sardonic bow, Will obeyed.

When they reached Laurel's chambers, her maids were ready with satin pillows piled high on her bed and a goblet of wine beside it.

Laurel still looked pale and weak as the duke eased her onto the pillows and smoothed her hair back from her high forehead.

"Shall I stay?" the duke asked in the thoughtful, loving voice Will remembered from childhood.

"Be gone, my lord. You are eager to go hawking." She laughed softly.

The duke looked up, and Will met the plea in his eyes. "I swear I will make her rest," he promised.

"I trust you in all things, Will." The duke nodded. "I shall return to find Laurel well once more." He placed a gentle kiss on her lips and stalked from the room.

"My lord cannot bear when I am ill." Laurel sighed. "Now you must sit by my side." Her smile trembling at the corners, she patted the edge of the satin-draped bed.

He sat close, as bidden, and held her cool, outstretched hand.

"Will, tell me your thoughts about Lady Elizabeth."

Before this day, he would have sworn he could share all with Laurel. Now sharp unease and heavy confusion caused him to choose his words with care.

"Lady Elizabeth is more beautiful than rumored."

"'Tis true!" Laurel sat up straighter. "I've never beheld such an abundance of curling, shining dark hair, nor eyes as light green as spring buds. I hope she will become my friend."

He tightened his grip on her hand. "All wish to be your friend, Laurel."

"Yes, I saw kindness on her face, yet I felt—" Laurel shook her head. "—such power around her. You felt it?"

From the moment their eyes met, nay, before, watching her walk with pride and strength toward them, he knew Elizabeth was coming to him.

He shook his head to clear it of traitorous thoughts and desires.

Not to me, to Carlyle.

"Lady Elizabeth has great pride and knows well how to behave as a future duchess."

"I hope she brings much merriment to our court and to our villagers, for they plan a fair in her honor." Laurel coughed and took a long, shuddering breath as if struggling to draw air into her lungs.

Will reached for the goblet of wine. "Drink."

"Nay." She shook her head. "I need it not. What I desire is to see young Stephen on the morrow. He is all I need to make me light of heart and health. As all he needs is a mother." Laurel slanted him a familiar worried look.

Sighing, he smiled, acknowledging her concern. "You know Stephen has his nursemaid, and you are a mother to him."

"Will, you are the brother I was never blessed to have, and I am a loving aunt to Stephen. Yet he needs more. A woman who will catch him when he stumbles. A woman you want always by your side."

I have found her and she belongs to another.

"Will, your face! What troubles—"

Laurel's sudden spasm of coughing cut his heart. He knew worse could follow.

"Call my grandfather," Will commanded the hovering maid.

"I am here." His grandfather spoke from the door and moved swiftly to take Will's place.

"Laurel, drink this potion I've prepared for you." Charles Grey held a cup to her pale lips and she clasped it with her palms, swallowing it in great gulps.

Sighing, she fell back on the pillows. "Truly in your hands, the magic of the old gods is good."

"There is no magic in the elements of our world. Air. Fire. Earth. Water. They are gifts to us to be used wisely."

"Your wisdom brings me much peace, Charles Grey," Laurel whispered, her eyelids drooping.

"Then rest and find more comfort, sweet Laurel."

Will and his grandfather stepped away, watching Laurel close her eyes. When her breathing became an even rhythm, his grandfather nodded.

"The plant I brewed will help her sleep. It grows in a part of the forest seldom visited by others." His grandfather stared deep into Will's eyes. "There I found signs of the old, dark pagan ways. The blood of the sacrifice was fresh upon the altar. Have your scouts heard rumors of the dark practices rising again to menace us?"

Instinctively, Will's hand went to his sword. He knew of the glade in the deep forest where such an altar had once stood. Long ago, when they were boys, Carlyle had shown him a special place he had found. It was an old memory he kept silent out of past love for his brother. For the love he still felt, he tried to ignore the cunning and depravity he sometimes sensed in Carlyle. If his brother had succumb to his fascination with the old, dark ways, he would discover the truth and put a stop to it for the sake of their father. *And to spare Elizabeth.*

Will lifted his chin and stared steadily back at his grandfather. "Have you spoken to the duke about what you have seen?"

His grandfather glanced back to Laurel, who slept peacefully now. "When her attacks of the lungs become less frequent, I shall burden him with the news. No need to spoil tomorrow's banquet to celebrate Carlyle and Elizabeth's betrothal." Watching him, his grandfather's eyes darkened. "What think you of the match, Will?"

The match is wrong! Elizabeth belongs to me! As he had done with Laurel, Will chose his words with care, fighting the powerful feelings pounding through him from the moment he saw Elizabeth.

"My brother is a fortunate man."

• • •

The pungent aroma from the flowers and herbs Florea kept thickly strewn across his chamber floor masked the sharp scent of blood.

Carlyle waited for her as he had every night in remembered time.

She appeared as if born of the shadows. Her long fingers stroked his hair, knew where his neck muscles corded with tension. He sighed, lifting one of her gnarled hands to his lips, kissing the rough flesh.

This was the hand, as strong as the sacred oak, which had held his fist clutching the jeweled blade for his first sacrifice to the old gods.

"My Flower, it is as you foretold. Elizabeth is marked by magic."

Florea's chuckle warmed his ear. "As you were marked by magic as a babe suckling at my breasts and learning the lore of our pagan gods in your nightly lullabies. All shall be as I promised."

He tensed. "When? I grow eager for my due all the old gods decree I should possess."

Again her fingers dug deep into his flesh, smoothing his bunched muscles.

"Elizabeth is young and pure of heart. She does not yet understand the great power she possesses within or wears wrapped about her body."

He twisted to gaze up at his old nurse. "Her celestial girdle is her source of power?"

"The power of the girdle can only be released by Elizabeth recognizing and accepting all she is destined to be." Florea cupped his face with hot palms. "You are destined to be the catalyst to release Elizabeth's darkness. With her by your side there is naught you cannot possess in the future."

The past flashed before his eyes. Will showing him how to fence with his first small rapier. Will, taller and stronger, teaching him to ride with the wind. Will, his strokes sure, helping him as he floundered clumsily while swimming in the stream. Always watching with indulgence and affection, the duke's eyes lingered on Will, never on him. Florea had helped him see the truth. She had guided and soothed him as admiration and fondness had dissolved into jealousy and scorn for his brother—and finally into a deep hatred for Will, whom all loved. None more than the duke, who could not hide his preference for this favored son. "In the future I shall have my father's respect above all others? There will be none to challenge me?"

She kissed his cheek. "Yes, Carlyle. As I made sure there would be no other heir to threaten what is rightfully yours, I promise at last you can vanquish your bastard brother."

Dunham Castle, 1601

My world spins around me, scattering my thoughts to the winds.

I have faced the danger my old nurse had foreseen. My choice, made in eagerness with my heart and soul, was unwise beyond my capacity to fully understand how I could so have lost my way.

A strong passion and deep longing I dare not have believed possible consumed me when I believed I had met my betrothed. I knew with him I had found my destiny.

Yet the man to whom I gave my heart in one look is not Carlyle, Earl of Seymour, heir to the Duke of Lennox.

The man is named Will Grey, Captain of the Guard.

Confronted by such feelings, I faltered, forgot all I have been taught. All I must do.

Now I must close my mind and heart to these traitorous longings.

I am Lady Elizabeth York, the Earl of Wharton's only child, and know well my duty.

Yet, even reason and purpose cannot still the questions burning in my mind.

Surely the blood of the duke runs through Will's veins. Yet I sense deep within me there is more to his story than him being a bastard son and grandson to the duke's physician. More which I crave to learn.

Who is Will Grey, and why do I know that our destinies are to be entwined for all time when duty demands it cannot be so?

Chapter Two

A sleepless night spent staring at the curved ceiling, searching for her compass, the sense of self which had always guided her, left Elizabeth fearful of meeting with Laurel this morning.

What if Will is with her and I falter as I did when first our eyes met?

Her chamber door swung open, startling Elizabeth out of her careening thoughts of Will and her future.

"What can you have been thinking not calling for me last night?" Snapping brown eyes wide, her maid Alice, sounding very much like her grandmother, Cybil, exploded into the room.

Pleased by the interruption, for indeed she felt only disgust with her new weakness and dishonorable desires, Elizabeth flung back the bed cover and rose. "You had fallen asleep. Fatigued by our long days of travel. I managed with the duke's servants."

Hands on hips, sensible Alice surveyed the damage done by Elizabeth's sleepless hours of soul-searching. "I can see the fine job they did by the look of you. Not even my Granny Cybil's concoctions can take away those purple shadows from under your eyes." Sighing, she shook her head, brown curls bouncing about her face. "Well, let me try to put all back as it ought to be."

Like she'd done since the first day, when they were both young girls giggling together, Alice helped Elizabeth through her morning absolutions.

Once dressed, she sat in front of the gilt-edged mirror to have her long, oft-unruly hair brushed. At last she caught a smile from Alice.

"Elizabeth, I know you are not fond of gossip but if you let me tell you what I learned last night and this morning in the kitchens, I won't be hurt by you not letting me do my duty. Such stories there are here and all eager to tell."

Curiosity and confusion had been her demons throughout the long night and they had not vanished with the dawn sun.

With a fearful determination, Elizabeth nodded. "It is no doubt wise to be informed about my new home."

"Indeed," Alice replied, a lilt in her voice. "Well, Carlyle's mother, Judithe, brought a great dowry and vast lands to the west, along the border."

Elizabeth knew well the role she played. "As I bring gold and lands to the east, with access to the sea."

"Well, let's hope that is all the two of you have in common!" Alice frowned. "Poor Lady Judithe. One year after she produced an heir in Carlyle, she again was with child. She endured months of illness before she lost the babe. It would have been another son to secure the lineage. She never recovered from the loss."

In the mirror, Elizabeth met Alice's eyes. "Surely Charles Grey could have helped her. He appears very wise in the ways of health and well-being."

"Lady Judithe would have no part of him. She only desired to be attended by a servant who had come with her from her home. She who was also Carlyle's nursemaid. Lady Judithe lingered for two years until one morning she simply did not awaken."

Remembering the loss of her own mother, Elizabeth took a deep breath. "Carlyle and I have a bond in both losing our mothers at too tender an age."

"There is more you need to know," Alice insisted. "The duke did not seek another bride. Then in the plague epidemic of '93, his old friend Sir George Douglas of Wyndham fell ill. He sent his daughter, Laurel, here for safety. The duke dispatched Charles Grey to Sir George's side, yet he could not save him. But he bore back to the duke from Sir George a last letter requesting his old friend to marry his beloved Laurel. And he bequeathed to him monies and small parcels of land to the south."

Alice took a large gulp of air to continue. "They say Lady Laurel and her father often visited here and she had long held the duke in high admiration. All believe it is a gentle, caring match for them both."

Such compassion touched Elizabeth. Her eyes misted and she blinked to clear them. "I sense great kindness in the duke."

"His Grace is much beloved by all. As is that handsome captain of the guard. It is plain the blood of the duke runs in

Will Grey. All know it is a great privilege and show of trust for the duke to bestow such a title upon him. There's a story there but none seems to know the truth of it." A determined gleam lit Alice's dark eyes. "I shall unearth the truth before I return to Wharton Keep after your wedding."

"No!" Elizabeth rose, stricken by the sure sense it was a betrayal of her feelings toward Will to discuss his secrets.

"No," she said more gently, embracing Alice. "Do not waste your time here on others. Enjoy yourself. I know it was difficult for you to leave your life and family at Wharton Keep, even for so brief a time."

"Aye, I long to return to them all, yet it was Granny Cybil who told me it was my destiny to come with you. None argue with her."

Again, Alice's sharp gaze traveled over Elizabeth's hair, now held high by ribbons. Nodding, she gave one last tug on the folds of Elizabeth's jade satin gown. "There now, you look more your beautiful self. I've been told you are to visit with Lady Laurel. Off with you. I shall make ready your bath and all you need for tonight's festivities."

Feeling more settled with trusted Alice by her side, Elizabeth hurried along the cool corridor to Laurel's chambers.

She swayed to a halt, her heart thumping against her ribs, meeting Carlyle helping an elderly woman who carried a bouquet of yellow field flowers. She was dressed as a servant but the indulgence plain on Carlyle's face proclaimed her much more.

"Ah, Lady Elizabeth, you have caught us," he said winsomely, slight color flushing his cheeks. "My old nurse, Florea, has picked these flowers for Laurel. Would you present the blossoms to her?"

Bowing, Carlyle's old nurse held the bouquet out. When Elizabeth took it she caught a milky glance from eyes no longer sharp to view the world around her.

"Florea is a beautiful name. Made of flowers," she said softly.

"Ah, Elizabeth, you understand why my pet name for my nurse has indeed always been *My Flower.*"

Florea's pale lips twitched into the semblance of a smile.

Witnessing Carlyle's kindness to his old nurse— mirroring Elizabeth's feelings toward her own Cybil— lessened her unease with him.

Yet another bond I share with Carlyle.

"Forgive me, Elizabeth," he said, with apology in his eyes. "I must leave you to lead Florea back to her chamber."

She stepped aside, watching him gently guild his old nurse away.

I must remember this kindness when I falter and think of naught but Will...

Feminine laughter and tiny giggles coming from Laurel's chamber brought Elizabeth back to this moment she had dreaded. Lifting her chin, she slowly entered the room which was hung with tapestries of gold and scarlet. Thick, ruby-colored carpets were strewn across the stone floor.

Still in her black silk night robe, Laurel lounged upon satin-and-velvet pillows placed on the floor where a small male child sat beside her.

Elizabeth bowed. "I come bearing gifts from Carlyle and his old nurse, Florea."

A servant appeared at Elizabeth's side, taking the heavy, sweet blossoms from her arms.

"Yes, leave them and come join us," Laurel called.

Obeying, Elizabeth walked toward the duo. The babe blinked up at her, his rosebud mouth curling to reveal two milk teeth and a dimple in his chin. Gurgling with laughter, he pushed himself up on pudgy legs, swayed, and took two unsteady steps toward her.

Elizabeth quickened her steps to catch him as he toppled forward. Cooing, he buried his face in the warm hollow between her neck and shoulder. His white-gold hair smelled of sunshine and soap.

Laurel clapped her small hands. "Look, Will. Young Stephen has gifted Elizabeth with his first steps. You have been properly welcomed to Dunham Castle."

Surprise and fear rushed through her, flaming across her skin. Gasping, she swung around to meet Will's gaze where he stood in the doorway. She hugged the babe more tightly to her breasts as if he could shield her from the powerful current pulling her toward him.

Desperate to break this strange hold Will had upon her, she turned back to Laurel. "Young Stephen is well favored."

Again, Laurel's light laughter echoed through the chamber. "He should be well favored. His father is the handsomest in the land. Only surpassed by my beloved duke."

His skin flushing, making his eyes even more startlingly blue, Will moved to Laurel's side.

Can this cooing child clasped in my arms be Will's son?

It felt as if she inhaled fire.

No. Will belongs to no other woman. He is mine.

Trembling with the strength of her confusion and desire, she carefully placed the babe back upon the floor. Instantly, his cornflower-blue eyes filled with tears. He stretched out his arms toward her, his mouth agape, and began to wail.

Despite all her resolve, her heart opened to him. She fell to her knees to again gather him close, rocking him.

A moment later, Will knelt beside her, reaching for his son. "I will take him, Lady Elizabeth."

Stephen clung to her, his pudgy arms tightening around her neck. "No, young Stephen, you must go," she whispered into his ear, his fragrant infant curls brushing her lips. "You need your mother."

"Stephen's mother died in childbirth." His face unreadable, Will swept his son away from her body, leaving her bereaved of his warmth. "Time for Stephen to rest. He awoke with the roosters."

Now seeing Will and Stephen cheek to cheek, Elizabeth recognized the man in the babe. She couldn't take her eyes from them as they left the room.

"Do not look so sad, Elizabeth. Their loss is a year past." Laurel's kind voice gave Elizabeth courage to ask the question burning through her heart and mind. A question which to her finely edged nerves did not feel like a betrayal of honor to ask.

"Will still mourns his wife?"

Laurel's moonbeam-fair, silky hair swung against her cheek. "Margaret was a sweet girl from a fine family but not a match of his making. The duke wished it for Will, and Will agreed out of love for him."

She fought to understand why her world was spinning out of control since her eyes had met Will's. *Why is my duty no longer as important as knowing more about Will Grey?*

Her eyes widening, Laurel patted the soft pillows, indicating for Elizabeth to slip down beside her.

"I see by your expression and your words that you are curious about Will. Here at Dunham Castle you shall hear many tales concerning him. Few are truly privy to the truth. If fortune smiles on you and you win Will's friendship, he may reveal himself to you. 'Tis not mine or any other's to tell."

Smiling, Laurel rose and pulled Elizabeth to her feet. "Come. I have a gift for you."

Feeling more unsettled about Will than when she had entered Laurel's chamber, Elizabeth waited, hiding her trembling hands in the folds of her gown.

A servant appeared from behind a heavy, crimson-colored curtain. Across her arms was draped a sapphire velvet gown with long, pointed sleeves and round décolletage edged with a thick ruffle of gold lace.

"Here at Dunham Castle we have heard many tales of the rich beauty of your celestial girdle. This gown matches the jewels. It will bring me great pleasure if you wear it tonight to the banquet to celebrate your betrothal to Carlyle."

At mention of her betrothal and all tonight meant, an icy chill spread from a deep coldness inside her. Again she fought it.

I shall not falter in my duty. I must forget Will Grey and remember I have seen kindness in Carlyle.

She clasped Laurel's hand and smiled. "This gown is as beautiful as you are generous. I shall wear it with pleasure tonight."

• • •

As promised, Alice had marshaled as many of the duke's servants as were needed to install an enormous copper tub in Elizabeth's new chambers. There, before the roaring fire, they heated buckets of water to fill the tub to half its depth. Above the imposing, steaming tub, placed neatly in a row on the mantle, were crystal jars of lavender, herbs, flower petals, fresh cream, and an odd-colored mixture which Alice breathed, "is known only as Granny Cybil's elixir of youth."

The duke's servants studied all the preparations with eyes round with either awe or curious speculation.

"Now off with all of you! I'll be attending Lady Elizabeth myself."

Amidst little gasps and shrieks of surprise, the other servants scattered away like dust in the wind.

Once alone with Alice, Elizabeth dropped her robe and stepped into the deep tub. Sighing with pleasure, she lay back, allowing the hot water to soothe her knotted muscles.

"Well, now, that's the bit. Relax while I wash your hair with Granny Cybil's formula." Alice frowned while mixing into a silver-rimmed bowl the proper parts lavender and her granny's magic elixir.

The concoction delighted the senses, a riot of floral scents that smelled like sunshine in the meadow, a fragrance Alice's nimble fingers picked up while massaging Elizabeth's scalp. Alice then poured cup after cup of water over Elizabeth's head until both were satisfied her hair was indeed clean and shining.

Her long, dark curls wrapped snugly in warm flannel and Alice scrubbing her body with rose petals and cream, Elizabeth at last allowed herself to reflect more calmly on her duty and the banquet ahead of her.

"Tonight will be a great celebration. I hope I do not disappoint the court," she murmured, gazing at Alice through hooded eyes.

"I have seen none at this court to compare to you. Even before I finish with you," Alice added with a grin.

Fatigued in body and spirit, Elizabeth gave herself over to Alice to scent her every curve and hollow. At last, she rose from the cooling water and dried in front of the fire. As she stared into the flames, her mind wandered to the duties she must perform tonight and how she must forget all else. Obediently, she allowed Alice to help her dress, standing before the long mirror as Alice patiently and skillfully wove sapphire velvet ribbons through her hair and coiled the famed celestial girdle around her hips.

They both stared at her reflection and Elizabeth admitted to herself that indeed the sapphire gown scooping low across her breasts, hugging her arms, and flowing down her thighs did cause the jewels of her girdle to sparkle with life.

As Alice had prophesied, no potion to enhance beauty could disguise the bluish shadows beneath Elizabeth's eyes from her restless night. She tried to mask the shadows with a smile and stood very still as Alice rubbed red rose petals into her lips to darken their color.

"Never seen you look more beautiful." Alice sighed.

I wish I knew if Will finds me beautiful.

She blinked away the image of him smiling at her in admiration.

"You do your father proud," Alice whispered, a catch in her voice.

Ruthlessly burying every other desire, Elizabeth straightened her shoulders. "I promise I shall forever strive to do so."

Her smile firmly in place, Elizabeth glided along the long corridor, guided by servants leading her to the vast banqueting hall and Carlyle.

He awaited her at the entrance, the wide, thick, dark doors open behind him showing a blur of moving bodies and exposing the strains of merry songs.

She refused to allow her smile to falter.

I shall remember all I have been taught. Remember Carlyle, too, has suffered losing a beloved mother. Remember his kindness with Florea. Remember that I must marry him for it has been decided by my father. It is my duty to obey and forget this madness which consumes me for Will.

She stretched out her hand to allow Carlyle to escort her inside.

"Ah, Elizabeth, bewitching as always," he murmured, stroking her wrist with his thumb. "Let the merriment begin."

She fought the shiver his touch sent along her skin as he led her into the banqueting hall. Torches blazed bright, casting long patches of light onto the jugglers, musicians, and dancers entertaining them. Through all the play of light and shadows, her gaze unerringly found Will and their eyes locked. As it had each time they met, the desire to go to him, to touch him consumed her. She fought it, deliberately looking away and up into Carlyle's face.

He smiled and with long, confident strides led her to the table and her place of honor next to the duke.

Her thoughts racing, her heart pounding, Elizabeth moved as if in a dream. The jewels worn by the many guests sparkled so brightly that they stung her eyes, and the musicians seemed to be playing songs which echoed in her head over and over, while the jugglers appeared to become bigger and then smaller before her. She blinked again and again, trying to determine if this night was real or if she would awaken in her bed at Wharton Keep, having dreamed it all

Even Will, the embodiment of all I have ever hoped to find in a man?

She felt the soft pillows at her back, tasted the wine cool on her parched throat, soothing as she drank. She smelled the roasting meat before her as dozens and dozens of main dishes were offered.

This was no dream, and she knew it. This was the future her father and the duke had decided for her and there was naught she could do to change it.

The thought brought such rage she stared down at her hands, clenching them together to keep from shaking with her feelings. Laurel's laughter brought her back to her duty. Taking a deep breath, Elizabeth looked up.

"My lord, it is now time for merriment." Laurel, radiant in silver, laughed up at the duke. "A wholesome recreation of the mind and body."

Smiling, the duke inclined his head toward the musicians who began playing the stately cords of the pavane.

With the duke and Laurel, Elizabeth and Carlyle led other members of the court into the center of the vast torch-lit hall.

As her dancing master at Wharton Keep had taught her, Elizabeth lightly touched fingers with Carlyle to follow the duke's lead, parading around the hall. The ladies of the court were a riot of color and of scents as they passed one another, flaunting their finery.

The advancing and retreating steps of the dance,

curtsies, brushing her foot forward to show a point of her jeweled slipper had been easily learned and practiced often at Wharton Keep. Carlyle comported himself well as she tried to disregard the long table where Will stood, watching the dancers.

She smiled at her betrothed and he back at her as it should be.

As it is destined to be.

When the music ended, Carlyle lifted her hand to his lips. "Are you disappointed?"

Elizabeth shook her head. "You are indeed a master of the dance," she said, speaking the truth.

He laughed, torchlight in his dark eyes. "We shall discover your feelings after the lively galliard, which usually follows and complements the pavane."

Laurel clapped her hands. "The Lavolta!" she commanded.

A breath of surprise whispered through the crowd.

Flicking Elizabeth an amused glance, Carlyle leaned closer. "Our Laurel is in high spirits this night."

Truth to tell, Elizabeth felt a jolt of surprise at sweet Laurel commanding a dance that had never completely been dignified since good Queen Bess performed it with the Earl of Leicester years ago.

The duke raised one eyebrow. "I grant you all indulgences. If you must perform the Lavolta, it needs be with the most accomplished dancer at court."

Elizabeth glimpsed the slightest hesitation before Laurel nodded. "You are right in all, my lord. My love of dance allows me to forgive your defection. Indeed, Carlyle is the finest dancer at court. Then who shall partner Lady Elizabeth?"

"Will," the duke commanded, motioning toward him.

The world spun blackly around her as the gods mocked her.

Hiding her trembling hands within the folds of her gown as she had done earlier in her storm of feelings about this night, these men, Elizabeth watched Will, his face utterly without expression, bow before the duke.

"Your Grace, I obey you in all ways. Yet I fear my talent is not for dancing. Lady Elizabeth's disappointment is assured."

Yes, Will, I pray you stop this madness! Why are the gods playing with us?

Laughing, the duke clasped Will's shoulder. "I fear for neither of you." With a wave of his large hand, the music began.

His eyes dark and his mouth a straight line, Carlyle gazed down at her. "I surrender you but this one time, Elizabeth," he murmured before taking Laurel's hand.

With no excuse possible, Elizabeth stood before Will to begin the most suggestive of all court dances.

Why have the gods decreed I shall soon be in his arms?

The thought of how she might feel, how she might falter, drove the blood from her heart.

Avoiding his eyes during the lively steps of the galliard, always the beginning of the *Lavolta*, gave her a moment to draw breath into her searing lungs.

Then Will's hand was on her back and she placed hers on his shoulder. They faced one another, both still refusing to make eye contact, as they turned slightly from side to side.

The inevitable moment came as she knew it must. Breathless, she sprang into the air and Will caught her, lifting her slowly up his body.

At last their eyes met and tears burned behind her lids.

This is as close as we shall ever be.

The feel of his hands on her body, his thigh against her thigh, made her softly sob with longing. She gasped, praying he had not heard.

"Do not be afraid, Elizabeth." His voice was strong, sure, and honeyed with kindness. "Here at Dunham Castle you will find friends who know your worth. Long have your loving ways to all at Wharton Keep been known to us."

Lost in the brilliance of his cornflower-blue gaze as he placed her gently back on the stone floor, she whispered the words beating in her heart and soul. "I wish you to be my friend, Will."

Mercifully, the dance separated them before he answered.

She knew not how she made it back to the table on trembling limbs, nor how she continued to perform her duties. She knew only gratitude that Will sat too far away for her to gaze at him with confusion and this fearful longing she must conquer.

The duke watched them all with the pride she'd often seen on her father's face. "You are pleased with all you find at Dunham Castle, Lady Elizabeth?"

Elizabeth thrust up her chin. "Yes, Your Grace. Very pleased indeed."

"We must afford Lady Elizabeth every desire of her heart." Carlyle smiled as he turned her hand over and kissed her birthmark.

The witches' mark at her wrist froze beneath his touch, the chill spreading through her body.

Why does his touch bring fear to my heart?

"My son speaks true. What do you enjoy, Lady Elizabeth, so we may provide it?"

Elizabeth tried to still the shiver deep inside her as Carlyle continued to stroke the birthmark at her wrist. She forced words from her tight throat.

"Riding is my greatest pleasure, Your Grace."

"Mine also." Smiling, Laurel looked around the duke. "We shall ride on the morrow."

A deep crease cut between the duke's wide eyes as he shook his head. "I must deny you, Laurel. I fear it will sap your strength and make you again unwell."

"My lord, Charles Grey urges me to breathe in the fresh air outside our castle walls." Laurel gave him a pleading expression and placed her hand on his arm.

Sighing, the duke covered her hand with his own wide palm. "So be it. Will, you must accompany them."

"I can accompany them, father," Carlyle drawled beside her.

"We meet with the council tomorrow." The duke nodded. "It must be Will."

Down the long narrow table, Will rose. His black cloak worn over one shoulder and gathered up over the arm secured by a sash was more somber than Carlyle's embroidered gold. And more striking for it.

She met Will's eyes, and to Elizabeth, the flickering torches seemed to throw all else into shadows except him. Again their gazes melded together, neither able to look away this time.

He bowed. "It shall be as you wish."

Will spoke the words for the duke, yet she sensed deep within her that he meant them for her.

A profound sadness settled into her soul as she sent him the silent message he already recognized.

My wish is not for friendship. My wish is for what we both know can never be granted.

Dunham Castle, 1601

The sun rose this day with laughter.

It came from Stephen, Will Grey's motherless infant son. Will's face and body haunts me and now his tenderness with his son, and the babe himself, has found a place in my heart. Both are beloved of Laurel and the duke. If only I could be a part of such a band of happiness. I cannot.

The sun set with a strange fear.

At the banquet to celebrate my betrothal to Carlyle, the duke commanded much merriment. I felt no joy but forbidden desire in the arms of Will as we danced.

And I sensed danger.

My shudders of fear come from my betrothed, Carlyle, despite the kindness I have seen in him for Florea, his old nurse. My feelings make me yearn for my Cybil's power to pierce the mists of time to see what is true. Is this, too, a choice my beloved nursemaid warned against? Because of being drawn to Will, am I choosing to poison all feelings toward Carlyle so when he touches me, peering down at my birthmark and smiling, I freeze with fear?

I know well the alliance between my father and the duke will bring much wealth and power to Wharton Keep.

I promise you, I shall purge myself of these foolish forebodings of Carlyle and feelings toward Will! My duty is to forge the right path for you who come after me.

Chapter Three

Since the day Will had been brought to Dunham Castle long ago, the duke had decreed they begin and end each day together. Before dawn, Will entered the duke's warm chambers to find him pacing, a sheath of letters clasped in his hands.

"What has happened?" Will asked sharply, concerned at the heavy lines in the duke's face and the slumped shoulders of the man he admired above all others.

His eyes weary, the duke turned. "Pray give me pleasure, Will, not such a frown to begin this day."

Knowing what was needed, Will smiled. "It is a fine morning for riding with the wind, your Grace."

"Yes, thanks be to you." The duke sighed, clasping Will's shoulder. "In you I see your mother's smile. It is much needed this day."

"Tell me what has happened?" Will asked again.

The duke spun on his heels to resume his pacing across

the rich blue carpets until he stood, legs wide apart, in front of the fire. The light cast by the blazing logs threw into relief the strong bones of the duke's face and his narrowed, worried eyes.

"In the good queen's reign we have been called upon to wage war with Spain, in Ireland, in France, and in the Netherlands. War costs money. The taxes levied in these last years have increased threefold. Harvests have been poor. Prices high. All make for desperate men." He lifted his fists, clutching the papers even tighter so his fingers whitened to their square tips. "The queen is old, unwell, and soon there will be new players on the board. James of Scotland will surely soon be King of England. Some say it will be a union of love between Englishmen and Scots. Others claim it shall be Catholic against Protestant. I say we here on the border between both must be ready and armed."

A fearful thought lodged in Will's mind and he became very still. "I know all of which you speak. We have spoken many times of the need to fortify our position. Unless a new play has been made to threaten us, why are you concerned now that the alliance with the Earl of Wharton has been forged?"

There was a slight hesitation and Will, seeing the answer on the duke's face, stiffened his shoulders to confront it.

"Will, do you believe my eyes are too old, my memories too faded to recognize longing and desire blazing as bright as the firmament? I tell you this again to remind us of our duty and soothe my conscience for being unable to give you what before God should be yours."

"I have never asked more of you than you have offered," Will answered in as unemotional a voice as he could muster, considering the hot, tight feelings warring within him since first his eyes met Elizabeth's. "I ask but one question. Knowing, why insist I ride with her this morning?"

In two strides his father reached him, the papers fluttering forgotten to the carpets as he gripped Will's shoulders with strong hands. "I would give my soul to have had one more minute with your mother. Allow me to give you this day."

Will lay caught within a net of pain and pleasure. He could cut himself free and flee in self-preservation. Or he could stay and continue to suffer exquisite torment.

Outside dawn had come and in a few hours he could see Elizabeth, if he so chose.

With unguarded eyes he met his father's steady gaze and nodded. "I promise I shall not forfeit this day."

The early morning autumn air tasted cold and crisp while the sun warmed Elizabeth's skin. Astride her horse, she galloped across the field, her long, cream-lined, crimson cloak billowing about her. She craved this freedom to clear the cobwebs of doubt about her future from her head and heart.

The wind carried the sound of Laurel's laughter and the strong, steady hoof beats of Will's black stallion.

"Race you both to the stream," Laurel called, her chestnut mare passing Elizabeth.

Taking the challenge, she urged her horse to lunge forward and the wind whipped her hair loose from its ribbons to flow behind her.

The earth trembled beneath them, the air thundering

with the power of their horses' gallops. At the edge of the woods, the clear, wide stream stretched before them as they halted next to it, the horses nose to nose.

Alive with laughter, the air sparked bright about them, filling Elizabeth with the joy and contentment of this moment.

Snorting, their breaths a light mist in the chill, the horses pawed the earth as Will pranced his black stallion around them.

The sun loved Will, kissing his strong cheekbones and lighting the blue of his eyes. "You both are well matched. I fought to keep pace with you."

A moment ago where contentment had blossomed, now arose an unstoppable primal urge, a part of her as elemental as drawing breath, which pulled her toward him. So close she saw herself reflected in his eyes, *felt* the heat of his body, she smiled up into his face. "Yes, Will. I am your match in all ways. Do we both not know it to be true?"

The answer of matched longing and desire, transforming the strong bones of his face and darkening his cornflower eyes to dark blue, terrified her with its power, yet urged her to say more, to hold this forbidden moment for as long as possible.

Somehow she felt his plea for reason, to save them both from more pain.

Biting her lip to keep it from trembling, she forced her horse to turn away from him. Out of the corner of her eye she caught a movement in the woods.

Three horsemen with swords drawn burst out from between the large oaks and galloped toward them. "Will!" she screamed.

Rapier drawn, he rode out in front of her, ready to attack the thieves before they could reach her and Laurel. The clash of steel as his blade met the first rider echoed in her ears.

Beside her, Laurel's chestnut startled and reared. Unable to stop the horse from bolting, Laurel screamed.

Her cry reached Will, and he wheeled toward them. "Go, Elizabeth! Help her," he commanded.

Heart pounding, holding her breath, she watched Will thrusting and cutting with his rapier, saw the second rider fall back before him. Only then did she obey.

Laurel's chestnut raced wildly across the rough ground. Elizabeth urged her horse to greater speed, felt grateful at being within reach of catching them at the bend in the creek.

Without warning, Laurel's mare again reared up, its eyes rolling in fear. Nearly there, Elizabeth stretched out her hand to help. Her face pale with fear, Laurel reached for her, missed, and tumbled off the bucking horse, striking her head on a rotting tree trunk.

"No!" Elizabeth screamed as she slid from her horse. She stumbled over the rough ground and fell to her knees at Laurel's side.

"Laurel, I am here to help you. I am here," she repeated over and over, stroking her face where blood streamed over her still features.

Elizabeth gathered up the hem of her cloak, pressing it against the gushing wound on Laurel's forehead.

Blood soaked through the cloth, staining the cream velvet lining, turning it red. Sobbing, she pressed harder, desperate to stop the flow which covered her hands and wrists.

Laurel's blood burned Elizabeth's birthmark until it

began to tingle.

The scalding tingling seeped through her skin, coursing through her veins, filling her mind with images and words. Whispers of old ways and the pagan gods who had forged her girdle to protect the women of her line.

Cybil had told her that someday she would understand the magic which lived within her. Elizabeth had feared the moment, wished for it never to come. Yet now, it called to her to help Laurel. Still fearful, still not understanding, she knew she must follow the commands whispering through her. With trembling fingers, Elizabeth pressed one of the jeweled crescents of her girdle against Laurel's wound.

In my hands, please let it heal her.

Slowly the deep cut closed, leaving a moon-shaped scar. As it did, her birthmark blazed hotter, glowing bright, until slowly it began to fade and cool.

The whispers told me true. In my hands the girdle has given me the magical power to heal Laurel's wounds.

Trembling with the knowledge, Elizabeth cradled Laurel in her arms, rocking her. Tears nearly blinded her. "Now please wake up...please wake up...please wake up."

Laurel's fair lashes remained a fan beneath her closed eyes.

Sobbing, Elizabeth felt for Laurel's heartbeat and the slow, soft breath coming from between her parted lips. *She lives!*

Gasping for air between her sobs, Elizabeth rested her cheek against Laurel's forehead. *Forgive me. My power is not great enough to awaken you.*

Terror a living force inside her, Elizabeth looked up, seeking Will.

Are you safe? Please, please, come to me.

Instead she found two more rough-looking, bearded men rushing out of the woods toward her.

Fear became a cold determination which gave her the strength to cradle Laurel in one arm and pull the tiny dagger from her girdle.

She felt the hoof beats of a galloping horse before she saw Will, brandishing his cutting sword, attack the men so very close to where she cradled Laurel in her arms. Once he appeared, all fear fled. As the primal knowledge of how to help Laurel had come to her, so did a deep certainty of Will's power and desire to protect her.

Ferocious in battle, he felled the first rider and engaged the second.

She held her breath as they clashed swords again and again. Will's great black horse reared and with one bold downward cut of his blade, Will vanquished the last thief.

A moment later, blood splattered on his leather jerkin, his face red and bruised, Will knelt beside her. His eyes searched her face and his hands roamed over her body as they had when they danced. "Tell me, did they hurt you? Are you harmed?"

"No," she swallowed a sob. "Laurel fell and struck her head. I cannot awaken her."

"Can you ride?"

She nodded, scrabbling to her feet as Will swept Laurel up in his arms. Mounting his horse, Laurel tight in front of him, he stared at Elizabeth, a question in his eyes. "Do I ask too much of you?"

"No. I shall keep up with you, Will," she promised.

Giving her no quarter, Will raced back to Dunham Castle

and she stayed by his side. The wind tore at her clothes and took away her breath. It hurt to draw air into her lungs, so full was she of terror for Laurel and a fearful acceptance of her newly discovered powers.

What am I and how should I use such enormous power and understand its limits and its price?

Reaching the guardhouse, Will waved to a young man with locks gleaming fiery red in the sunlight. "Tom, summon my grandfather!" he commanded.

"He is in the castle!" Tom shouted back, turning to follow orders.

Trailing Will through the long corridors, Elizabeth ran to keep up with his powerful strides as they entered Laurel's chamber.

Her maids gasped, their faces frightened.

"Loosen your mistress's clothing," he commanded and placed Laurel gently on the bed.

A wave of unfamiliar darkness swept over Elizabeth's sight and she swayed, trying desperately to stay erect.

Will caught her, his warm hand cupping her neck beneath her hair, fallen loose in their mad ride. "Forgive me. I pushed you too hard."

Once again so close to him, Elizabeth fell silent, only watching his eyes as he gently seated her on the chair beside the bed.

What might my powers mean for the two of us?

The door burst open and Charles Grey, carrying a black leather box, hurried into the room.

Will turned away to speak softly to his grandfather. "Laurel fell from her horse and struck her head. She has not awakened."

Elizabeth watched Charles Grey carefully examine Laurel, so still and pale upon the bed. He paused, rubbing his fingertips slowly over and over the crescent scar on her forehead. "This is new."

Their eyes met, and she saw knowledge in his.

Somehow he knows the magic I performed.

The pounding feeling of being pulled down a path both welcome yet frightening weakened her as she held his wise gaze.

"Stay here, Lady Elizabeth," he said quietly. At last he looked away and up at his grandson. "Will, it must be you who summons the duke to tell him I shall restore Laurel to him. Then he will believe."

With a nod, Will hurried from the room.

"Now, Lady Elizabeth, I will prepare an elixir. You must help me force Laurel to swallow it." From his black box he pulled out three bottles of different-colored liquids. He mixed two into one until the fluid began to turn a light green and then bubbled to the top of the vial.

Elizabeth rose, motioning the maid away. Taking her place, Elizabeth held Laurel's shoulders and head up so Will's grandfather could slowly carefully spoon the thin liquid between her pale lips.

"Yes. That shall do." He sighed, placing the bottle back into his box. "Now we must let her rest."

His face ashen, the duke ran into the chamber and fell to his knees beside the bed. "Laurel, my dear. I am here with you." He grasped one of her small hands between his wide palms.

Torn between giving the duke and Laurel privacy and her burning desire to stay in this room to help in any way she could, Elizabeth waited for a sign to tell her what to do.

She felt Will's power and heat before he placed a goblet of wine on the table beside her.

"Here, Elizabeth. Drink this for strength. You are pale and trembling. I sense you wish to stay."

"As you will stay," she said softly, lifting the goblet still warm from his hands to her lips.

Elizabeth ached at the firm set of Will's jaw and the anguish in his eyes as he watched the duke bending his head over Laurel, kissing her bruised brow.

"Yes," Will said, "I will stay."

"Then we shall stay together." Their eyes met and again she saw the forbidden desire which quickened her heart beat.

Yes, Will. I too feel a need to steal these moments together which frightens us both.

"Yes, Elizabeth, we will stay here together. For Laurel."

He took a stance before the door as if to fight off everything or anyone who might enter this safe, loving haven they were creating.

His grandfather turned away from the bed. "Will, it shall be a long day and even longer night. You have other duties to perform for the duke."

His gaze sweeping over the room, lingering on her face, Will hesitated for three painful beats of her heart. She caught her breath when, with a curt nod, he turned, stalking out.

"You must also take your leave, Lady Elizabeth." Charles Grey lifted her hand, urging her from the chair.

Shaking her head, she glanced at the duke kneeling beside the bed.

"We will help both Laurel and his Grace by giving them privacy. Rest and return later with your strength and kindness."

Fatigue, fear, and confusion warring within her, Elizabeth gazed into Charles Grey's eyes. His steadiness gave her strength and she nodded. "Yes. I understand what you need from me, and I shall do as you ask."

Dunham Castle, 1601

I have begun a journey beyond any I could have deemed possible.

I am only now beginning to understand the power of my birthmark and what lives within me. My old nurse, Cybil, told me false. I must be a witch, for in my hands, my celestial girdle has the power to heal. Yet I am not all powerful, for I cannot awaken Laurel from her sleep.

I pray to learn how to use these magical powers I have been given. And I yearn to understand how I can control my desires to be one with Will Grey instead of with my betrothed, Carlyle.

I feel as if I am wandering through a waking nightmare where I do not know which way to turn to awaken. I pray soon the way shall become clear for all of us.

Chapter Four

In silence, Alice helped Elizabeth bathe in scented water, gently washing away the blood and filth of her ill-fated ride. Nothing could cleanse her feverish thoughts.

"What can I do to help you?" Alice asked quietly, her spirit seemingly subdued by the tragedy.

"I don't know what to do," Elizabeth whispered, her gaze studying the celestial girdle and the mark of magic on her wrist.

What powers do you possess which I must yet learn? How might I still help Laurel?

"I know you wish Granny Cybil was here." Alice sighed, her gaze on Elizabeth's birthmark. "She has the eye to see what's to be done. All I can do is make you ready for whatever might come and remind you that Granny Cybil says magic has its price."

Alice's words ringing through her head, Elizabeth allowed her long hair to be brushed until it cascaded freely about her shoulders and down her back. Frightening thoughts and unanswered questions quickened her breath, making the air feel stale and heavy in her chambers.

"I can't breathe in here."

Nodding, Alice set down the brush. "Aye. Fresh air is what you need."

Suddenly eager to be out of doors, Elizabeth carefully wound her golden girdle over her loose cream gown and fled, leaving Alice alone.

Elizabeth made her way outside, into the dying afternoon which threw shadows upon the dusty apron of the courtyard surrounded by a bake house, brewery, barns, and stables.

She spotted Will, his hair gilded by the setting sun, as he stood surrounded by his men. She stayed in the shadows to watch him, his beautiful face animated, as he spoke to the young soldier who had been on watch at the castle wall. She caught snatches of their conversation. "Tom…training… troops…border."

When Will moved to examine a horse the blacksmith brought to him, the red-haired young soldier's eyes followed, worship on his young, freckled face.

Will moved among all the men working in the courtyard. He gripped the armorer by the shoulder, patiently pointing out defects in the shield. He gave a quick smile and an approving nod to the farrier.

Here was a leader who was buffing his men like diamonds to be shining instruments for the duke.

Yet another great wave of longing for what could never be between them and a desperate rebellion against that fate swept over her. *Could my magic make him mine? What price would I be willing to pay to be with him?*

Tears stinging behind her eyes, she forced herself to turn away before she flung herself at his feet so desperate was her need for him.

Don't go, Elizabeth.

Her birthmark burned, her celestial girdle tightened around her body, commanding her to swirl back to answer him.

For some time Will had known Elizabeth watched from the shadows. He'd tried not to react, tried to perform his duty with his men. Until she turned to leave and an aching desire for her to stay swept over him.

Don't go, Elizabeth.

As if she heard his thought, she turned back to meet his gaze.

Her eyes darkened to the deepest green of the forest as he moved to where she stood in the shadows beneath the outer gallery.

Honor demands I send her away.

"The cold of night is falling, Lady Elizabeth. You should return to the warmth of the castle."

All the living color drained from her exquisite skin. "Did you not ask me to stay, Will?"

Only with my mind and heart. "Nay, I did not call out to you." The air between them beat with emotion. He fought it, squaring his shoulders, knowing duty demanded he defeat these traitorous desires.

"*I give you this day,*" his father had said and Will had promised not to forfeit it. Until Fate had decreed otherwise.

She began to shiver and he ripped off his short cloak to place around her shoulders.

"I will escort you to your chambers. You need to rest after a day such as this one. I fear it shall be a long night for us all."

"You also should rest, Will." She slid him a side glance, clutching his cloak to her body as she followed him. "You have worked hard with your men this day. As you fought hard to protect Laurel and me. You saved our lives," she ended softly.

"I would give my life to do so, Lady Elizabeth."

She looked up at him, her skin again alive with color. "I know it is your duty as captain of the guard. Nonetheless you have my gratitude. The duke is fortunate to have you by his side."

Her words struck old chords of faithfulness and love. "As I am fortunate to be able to give him my sword and my loyalty. My honor is all I possess."

He barely acknowledged the servants passing them in the long corridors as the tower bell tolled the hour.

From the first moment he saw her, Elizabeth's beauty had bewitched him, blocking out sane reasoning. Now her intoxicating scent filled his senses and her strength, spirit, and kindness made him long for the impossible. He knew he needed to quicken his stride, needed to return her safely back to where she belonged, but he could not when she strolled so slowly, her eyes searching his face.

"We are both bound by our honor. I wonder if there is not more to bind us all. Something more powerful."

At the door of her chamber she turned to him and slowly removed his cloak from her body. She held it out to him, but when he reached to take it, she held fast, staring into his eyes.

"I will remain with Laurel throughout this night. Let us pray the dawn brings answers for us all."

Motionless, his cloak in his hands, he watched her close her chamber door.

Love for family demanded he watch over Laurel. Honor demanded he resist his own desires.

Yes, Elizabeth, I have seen what is more powerful than honor and it brought much heartache. I can and shall spare you such pain.

Elizabeth sat beside Laurel and, as Charles Grey had foretold, the night stretched long as they kept vigil in the quiet warm bedchamber.

The candles had been replaced many times, as had the logs in the fireplace, when Will's grandfather clasped the duke's shoulder. "Laurel will awaken at dawn. Do not let her open her eyes upon your haggard face lest she worry. Rest. Word will be brought to you when all is well."

The two older men locked gazes. "Charles, you told me when you could not save our beloved Maude. And you spoke true when we lost Will's bride. I believe you now, my old friend."

Charles Grey stroked Elizabeth's hair. "You should also rest, child."

She smiled and shook her head.

Not until Will rests.

Charles Grey hesitated, as if to speak, before he looked to his grandson who was clasping the duke's shoulder. "As

Will is determined to stay." He nodded. "Come, your Grace, a few hours of slumber will serve us both well."

Once the two men were gone, Will sent away the servant and turned to her.

"Elizabeth, my grandfather is right. You should retire to your own chamber. Sleep and when you awaken, it shall be as my grandfather promised."

They were the first words he had spoken to her since their fraught walk back to her chamber and the strange occurrence in the courtyard when she realized she had not heard him call to her with her ears, but with her mind. Then, as now, it seemed as if the very air they breathed was alive with feeling.

She clasped her arms around her body to stop shaking. "I shall rest when you do. I want to stay. Laurel is also my friend."

Please don't make me leave you. I must soon enough. Let us have these few hours.

As if he could hear her thoughts as she had his, his mouth curled slightly. "I understand. You have become dear to Laurel's heart."

Cherishing these moments, she helped Will cradle Laurel higher on the pillows as he gently spooned more liquid between her lips and smoothed her fair hair back from her forehead.

The faintest blush of dawn brought with it a strong, chilly breeze. Elizabeth shivered and again he gazed into her eyes. "Elizabeth, please rest."

Stubborn, determined to steal time, she shook her head. "I shall rest when you do, Will."

Their eyes met and here in this quiet, darkened room,

where Fate had led them, Elizabeth did not need a sign to guide her. At last she knew what she must do.

She slid closer to him on the edge of Laurel's bed. "I know you are the duke's son. Yet I also know there is more to your story. Laurel said you might one day share the truth."

Will glanced lovingly at Laurel and back to stare unflinchingly into Elizabeth's eyes. "Even with so short an acquaintance, both my son and Laurel trust you. As I choose to do."

Barely breathing, Elizabeth was mesmerized by Will's strong profile in the flickering flames from the deep fireplace.

"My mother, Maude, was my grandfather's only child. She and the duke grew up together. Fishing in the streams. Playing in the woods. Helping my grandfather gather plants for his potions."

Will stopped, then sat quite still for a long time, staring into space. Moved by the strong emotions flashing through his eyes, she touched his shoulder. The sad smile he gave her broke her heart into tiny pieces.

"They fell in love. Even though my father was betrothed to Carlyle's mother, promising a great alliance which would bring power and more wealth to Dunham Castle, he told my mother he would defy the old duke. Alone late one night in the village church, my mother and father declared their love and commitment to one another. After their night together, my father went to the old duke and told him that he and my mother had declared their love before God."

Will shook his head. "The old duke would not be thwarted. He reminded my father of his lineage. The pride of his royal blood. My father returned to my mother, still declaring his undying love but reconciled that he must honor his blood and marry another."

A fathomless ache welled up inside her. "What happened?"

"My mother declared he had betrayed their love and she swore she would never see him again. So great was her pride that my father could not sway her. They never spoke again until the winter of my fifth birthday."

"Then she forgave him at last?" Elizabeth asked, wishing it with her whole being.

Will's eyes glistened like blue flames in the firelight. "That winter many were falling ill and dying. When my father learned my mother was sick, he came to my grandfather's house. Still she refused to see him. I remember him pacing outside her chamber door, pleading with her to let him enter. I remember him holding me tight in his arms, his tears wetting my hair. At last on the tenth day she called for him."

"Please tell me they had more time together," Elizabeth whispered, tears pooling at the back of her throat.

Will smiled gently. "My mother never stopped loving my father, nor he her, and so they confessed to one another. My father begged my mother to allow him to have a part of her in me. He wished to bring me to Dunham Castle. The last time I saw my mother, my father had climbed into her bed and she lay cradled into his body as if they were one. She died in his arms."

Sorrow greater than she'd ever known ripped her apart and she buried her face in her hands, sobbing.

"Elizabeth. Please. No tears."

She heard the concern in his voice, felt his touch on her shoulder.

A portal only he could fill opened inside her.

She threw herself onto his warm, hard chest, and his powerful arms closed around her.

"Do not weep, Elizabeth. It happened long ago."

"To have had such a love"—she sobbed, swallowing tears—"and to have lost it is a tragedy of the soul." She flung back her head, resting it on his shoulder, and gazed up at him. "In God's eyes you are the duke's firstborn son. I should be yours."

He slid his fingers into her hair, holding her still as he stared into her eyes. "I too feel this great power between us. That is why I told you my mother and father's story. So you would understand why I must protect you from such pain when the path of honor is not followed."

Within her, every feeling exploded in one desire. "Then give me this moment, Will."

He held back but she refused to surrender. She pulled him closer until with a sharp intake of breath he bent his head, seeking her mouth.

Her body felt made of hot light, radiant, as their mouths clung together, breaking, meeting, again and again.

Leaving her aching lips, he tasted the tears shimmering on her lashes and touched the pulse beating at her warm throat, and returned once more to her open, waiting mouth.

She had waited a lifetime, for surely this moment had been written in their stars.

With him she was a creature of light, spinning through galaxies, illuminating the heavens.

When they finally broke apart, she could barely pull the air in and out of her tight lungs.

Instinct and aching hunger caused her to cling to him. "No. I want more."

His mouth hovered above hers, and she coaxed his lips apart, craving the honey taste of him.

At last he dragged her tighter to him, deepening their kiss. In this newfound sensuality she twisted into his body, absorbing the hard muscles of his chest against her soft breasts.

Will's breathing quickened as his lips stroked over hers. Her heart seemed to swell in her chest, her blood pooling in her lower body as his experienced touch brought her head back to open her throat to hot kisses which fed her need but did not quench it.

"Elizabeth...we must stop." His voice sounded strange and far away, fading in the pounding need consuming her.

She opened her eyes and over his shoulder she saw Laurel watching them.

"You have awakened," Elizabeth gasped in confusion and relief. Trembling, bereaved to lose his warmth, she forced herself to twist away from Will to clasp Laurel's cool hand.

"I'll bring the duke." Will's voice sounded husky before he turned to stride from the room.

Eyes wide and searching, Laurel tightened her grip on Elizabeth's hand. "I remember but bits and pieces of what happened after my fall. It is as a dream. Yet now I heard and saw all clearly. As I saw the power between you and Will while we rode. What shall you do?"

Conflicting emotions and unfamiliar, frightening need still pounding through her body, Elizabeth shook her head. "We as women are but pawns in this game of kings to be moved about on the chessboard for gain of land or money. Or the need to carry on the family name or the linage to start or end wars. How can I change my destiny? And is it just if I should try?"

"I was a fortunate and eager pawn, for I had long loved the duke. I have been blessed to receive great affection and kindness from him," Laurel whispered. "Yet his feelings for me are as nothing compared to his great love of Will. There is little the duke would not grant him."

Laurel didn't say the words, yet Elizabeth read them in her eyes.

Even deny his legitimate heir and allow Will and me to be together?

Her father's face flashed before her. Again she heard the pride and pleasure in his voice when he declared to those gathered at Wharton Keep that she would one day be the Duchess of Lennox. Again she heard her old nurse warning of danger should her choices not be wise.

How can choosing Will and his love be unwise when it feels like my true destiny?

In a lifetime of loving obedience to his father, Will had never wished for more than Lennox had bestowed upon him. Now Elizabeth stirred emotions and desires which defied everything he had ever believed possible.

The joy on the duke's face as he roused him and led him back to Laurel's chamber lightened Will's heart. He lingered outside the chamber door, watching Elizabeth, remembering the feel of her body in his arms, the taste of her skin and lips.

He straightened his shoulders. He had not forfeited the gift of this day but the pride and the loyalty he owed his father demanded he must now stay away from her. Must somehow destroy these feelings, this bond which connected them more completely than anything he had ever known.

"The delicate Laurel lives, I see," Carlyle drawled behind him.

Aware of his brother's fear that Laurel would produce another heir after all, Will turned, taking a protective stance before the door.

Carlyle laughed. "Fear not, brother. I wish your sweet Laurel no harm. I have new plans. My bride brings a richer dowry than any know."

Unable to stop himself, Will again gazed at Elizabeth and back to his brother.

"Ah, you have fallen under Lady Elizabeth's spell." Carlyle laughed. "I am forced to share much with you, brother. Not her. I have special plans for the beautiful Elizabeth."

Although Will had always held his suspicions close and mourned the loss of the bond he had once shared with Carlyle, the time had come when he could no longer ignore the festerings of jealousy and cruelty which lured beneath his brother's charming exterior. Now finely attuned to Elizabeth with a fierce desire to protect her, he could no longer silence his fears or assuage his guilt that he had played a part in placing her in possible danger.

"Carlyle, there are rumors stirring of dark practices in the area. An altar has been discovered with evidence of sacrifices. If true, it could harm us all at Dunham Castle. I will not allow those I love to be placed in danger."

Carlyle's eyes widened and his mouth twisted in a smirk of contempt. "Do you believe I have knowledge of such a place or of those who worship the old gods? Big brother, you have always been too full of pride and love of our father to tell him or others of my boyhood fascination with the old ways. Why would you now speak of it to me? As before, we both know you would never betray your blood."

Will did not stop Carlyle from walking away nor did he warn him.

Do not give me reason to betray my blood, brother. For I swear to protect Elizabeth I shall defy all in my way.

Even his own blood.

Dunham Castle, 1601

Here in my new home, my world continues to take on new shape, new color, filling me with emotions I can no longer contain. I am confused and frightened by the power my golden celestial girdle granted me to heal Laurel's wound. I know my gift is not all powerful, but what can be its scope? And what might be its price? How may it help me reach my heart's desire with Will?

His grandfather is the one who caused Laurel to awaken, recovered except for a weakness in her limbs. Even this Charles promises to mend.

In the long, dark hours, as Will and I sat beside Laurel's bed, my world changed forever when he told me his true story.

Told me of the great love his mother Maude—Charles Grey's only child—and the duke pledged before God.

Told me of the tragedy of pride and duty which kept them apart yet never destroyed their love for one another.

In the eyes of God, then, Will is the duke's firstborn son. In my heart and soul I know I belong with Will.

Yet, in our world, it is Carlyle to whom I am betrothed.

Is it my destiny to right this injustice?

Do I follow my heart which yearns for Will in all ways a woman can love?

Or do I honor my father, the pride in his bloodline, and perform my duty as I have promised? I confess to you that I begin to dare to defy the teachings of my lifetime to carve out my own destiny.

In this, you shall judge me.

Chapter Five

The following two days, Will dutifully supported his father and attended Laurel in her chambers when she wanted him by her side.

And always beside her sat Elizabeth.

Elizabeth with the silky hair which always invited his touch. Elizabeth with the green eyes which seemed to look through his flesh and bones into his heart. Elizabeth, whose scent intoxicated the air he breathed.

Anguish grew with every moment when Carlyle made his daily visit and stood too close to Elizabeth, touching her.

Then Will would leave, driven by his desire to challenge his own brother. To challenge the dictates of his own conscience and his very honor.

On the third day, he entered Laurel's chamber to find her standing on her feet, supported by Elizabeth, her nightgown hanging in spreading folds to the ground. Squinting, his grandfather nodded. "Yes, my salve is helping."

"Look, Will! I showed my lord but an hour past. Now I must show you. Your grandfather's magic has brought life back to my numb legs." Tears in her eyes, Laurel gently eased away from Elizabeth and took three unsteady steps toward him.

She swayed and Will reached out to grab her, as did Elizabeth. In her attempt to help, she innocently pressed her lush, warm body into his.

He saw frank desire light her eyes as he had in those forbidden stolen minutes in Laurel's chamber. He lost pace with his breathing. His nerves were shocked and burned beneath his own hard desire which had increased with each day.

"Enough for today, Laurel. Time to rest." His grandfather stepped between Will and Elizabeth to help Laurel walk slowly back to her bed.

Elizabeth lifted her shadowed eyes to stare at him. "Will…" she said huskily.

Loud applause shocked them all into turning toward the door. Carlyle strolled into the room.

"Magnificent, Laurel. You have surprising resilience for one with such a delicate constitution."

Laurel's wavering smile tore at Will's already bruised heart. "Laurel is very brave," he declared to his brother. Blue steel meeting dark, their gazes clashed before Carlyle moved to Elizabeth's side, taking her hand to kiss her wrist.

"Now that our sweet Laurel is recovered, we must continue the celebrations for our wedding." Slowly he ran a fingertip along the delicate bones of her face.

Common sense told Will to remove his hand from his sword hilt and step away to calm his pounding need to protect Elizabeth from his brother.

It was she who stepped away, shaking her head. "I feel I should still stay by Laurel's side until she is fully recovered."

Will *felt* Elizabeth's tension from across the room and cursed the fact he could do nothing to ease it.

Pain gripped his gut as he remembered how he had been used to put her in this harm's way. Long had he suspected Carlyle of cruelty and vices, yet he had been eager to offer the unknown Elizabeth York for her money and the power behind her lands into such a man's keeping.

It is no balm to my conscience that it was done for the betterment of the linage. Does any man have the right to order another's life in such a way?

"Yes, Carlyle is correct." The duke's long strides carried him quickly into the chamber and to Laurel's side. She stretched out her hand and he held it, his eyes scanning each of their faces. "The fair in honor of the wedding must proceed. The people need a reason to celebrate. They need to feel safe and share in our happiness at this great alliance."

Will watched Elizabeth, wanting to somehow give her his strength.

Eyes shadowed, she nodded. "I understand, your Grace. When do you wish us to attend?"

"There is no need to wait longer. The sky is to be full of stars this night."

Laurel laughed softly. "My lord speaks true, Elizabeth. It will give me pleasure to think of you at the fair. Such a merry place full of wondrous sights." She glanced up at the duke. "You must also attend with Elizabeth and Carlyle, my lord."

"No, my dear, I shall stay with you," He lifted her hand to his lips.

"I would also like to stay," Will said quietly, meeting his father's steely eyes.

His father did not offer this night, nor did Will ask for it. Solemn, the duke nodded. "Yes. Your lieutenant shall accompany them."

Knowing his father well, knowing he was again reminding him that duty must prevail, Will conquered every movement, every expression, not wanting to betray his decision. Tonight he would tell his father his true thoughts. He glanced at Elizabeth's profile, she held her chin high, her back straight. Tomorrow he would fall on his knees before her asking forgiveness for leaving her, for casting away this gift between them of a love he never dreamed possible. Ask for forgiveness for not fighting for her as his heart told him he must while his honor forbid it. He felt his grandfather's eyes watching him and, turning, saw that Charles Grey already knew what had to be done.

Triumphant, Carlyle impatiently awaited Florea in his chamber. He dampened the fire to embers and snuffed all but a few candles.

Out of the darkness she materialized. He lifted one of her hands, squeezing it between his palms. "You saw true. My father is eager to continue the festivities for the wedding. The alliance must be forged. Elizabeth and I are to attend the fair this night."

Florea's thin lips curled. She nodded. "Present her with this."

He took the nosegay of tight purple flowers and blood

red berries he didn't recognize. Curious, he raised it to his nose, breathing deeply.

The fragrance surrounded him, filling his senses with bliss. He chuckled. "A love potion?"

"Tell Elizabeth it will keep away the stink of the animals and the foul smell of others at the fair. In truth it will cause her to see the world in brighter colors and be open to the feelings of others around her. To you, Carlyle." Florea stroked his arm. "Dazzle her with your charm, of which you possess much." She pressed closer, her words soft yet firm. "The old gods have shown me that on the day after the morrow, you must take her to the sacred place. There you must show Elizabeth your true self and she will discover that which is within her."

Excitement coursed through him and it was not the nosegay which made him burn with love for this old woman.

"Thanks to my Flower." He gently kissed her cold, dry lips. "Because of the love you bear me, I shall at last possess all the power I deserve."

As the duke had declared, the star-filled sky was a bright canopy for the fair as Alice and Elizabeth entered the festivities. Behind them paced Carlyle and the red-haired soldier Elizabeth now knew was Tom Chatham, Will's lieutenant.

It should be Will here with me. Why did he choose to forfeit these bittersweet hours we could share?

"I say again, I see no reason to carry the thing. The sights, sounds, and smells of the fair are the fun of it." Alice, sensible to her fingertips, gazed with narrowed eyes at the nosegay Elizabeth carried.

With her tired mind and stricken heart Elizabeth had not been clever enough to come up with an excuse when Carlyle had offered it.

She held the nosegay at arm's length and also eyed it with disfavor. "It is pretty enough. What is it that bothers us so about it?"

"The berries!" Alice shouted and then glanced behind her, as did Elizabeth. The men were in discussion about the strength of the troops and appeared not to have heard.

"Good." Alice sighed. "Would not want to embarrass Carlyle, but those berries look like the sort Granny Cybil once showed us to always avoid."

Elizabeth studied a blood red, irregularly shaped berry. "I remember. The ones which make you see the world false."

"Couldn't be, of course. Yet." Before Elizabeth could stop her, Alice whisked the nosegay from her hand, disposing it neatly in a bucket of slop at the edge of a shed holding sows. "If it is the berries, those will be the happiest pigs in the kingdom."

As they were being buffered by fairgoers and vendors shouting out their wares, Carlyle did not seem to notice the loss of her gift.

Satisfied, Alice turned her attention to the atmosphere of gaiety surrounding her.

To Elizabeth, her senses sharpened by confusion about these magical powers she seemed to possess and a growing rebellion against her fate and Will's, the fair spread out before her like a nightmare prism of animals and people trying to sell her everything from false gold to puppets to hot pies. The aroma of strong beer and sizzling food caused her stomach to gently stir in distress.

She stiffened her resolve and lifted her chin when Alice hesitated at the toy stall. Her face was as bright as a new penny. She picked up a rattle, gave it a good shake, and chuckled at the loud, jarring retort. "This can serve for my sister Jane's new babe." She slid Elizabeth a sly look. "Jane won't be thanking me for it."

Elizabeth smiled, knowing the sisterly rivalry which existed between them.

Suddenly at her side, Carlyle stiffened, frowning down at Elizabeth's empty hand. "Where is your nosegay?"

Feigning surprise and distress, Elizabeth glanced around. "I must have dropped it making my way through the crowd." In way of an apology, she clutched his arm, holding it to her side. "The fair is as wondrous as Laurel promised. Shall we continue?"

He stared down at her for two thumps of her heart before he smiled, shifting so their bodies touched more firmly. "Yes. The dancing is ahead."

Tom took possession of the rattle as far as the next booth, where they were met by the delicious aroma of cinnamon, figs, and ginger.

"Granny Cybil swears sucking on pieces of ginger aids digestion," Alice declared and promptly bought a bag of it.

Heroically, Tom also bore that parcel, a bundle of lace, and two sets of playing cards, one of which Alice planned to send back to Wharton Keep, along with the annoying rattle.

Watching Alice's progress though the fair lightened Elizabeth's heavy heart, making it possible for her to smile and to not cringe away when Carlyle touched her shoulder or their bodies brushed tightly together in the hustle of the merrymakers.

How different my feelings would be if it was Will by my side, as I know he surely is meant to be.

"Oh, look! There are the acrobats," Alice gasped, obvious delight on her face.

They watched with awed disbelief at the five men performing their leaps and contortions. Even Carlyle appeared amazed by their tricks.

Laughing, his face looking younger, he held her arm to lead her deeper into the festival.

She heard the lute, fiddles, and recorders being played with great energy before they reached their destination.

Couples were dancing in a rectangle, their steps much simpler and less intricate than those performed at court.

"I prefer dancing the Black Nag or the Petticoat Wag, but this one be a bit of fun." Eyes bright, Alice watched the dancers and tapped her foot in rhythm.

Elizabeth caught Carlyle's eyes and sent a silent plea.

He smiled. "Tom, I shall hold those packages. I believe Maid Alice would like to dance."

Almost before Tom had made the transfer of gifts into Carlyle's waiting arms, Alice grabbed his hand, pulling him into the rectangle of dancers.

In the torchlight surrounding them, Alice's brown curls shone, bobbing about her face, as nearly as red as Tom's hair.

Again Elizabeth sought Carlyle's eyes. "That was very kind of you, my lord."

"I can be, you know," he said in the same winsome voice he had used when she'd come upon him with Florea.

Guilt weighted heavily on her for all the rebellious plans

whirling through her mind to avoid marrying him so that she could be with his brother.

"That I will come to discover. I know you are a fine dancer and I shall enjoy your skill again tonight." She smiled with what she hoped was encouragement, for she knew the villagers expected a dance from the betrothed couple.

Still holding hands, and their faces split in wide grins, Alice and Tom rejoined them. Immediately Carlyle transferred the packages, took Elizabeth by the hand, and led her into the circle of dancers performing the Branie.

Carlyle's sideways steps, his every movement, were done with skill and grace.

She hoped she was comporting herself as the villagers expected and deserved, for her mind was not on the dance steps, but on Carlyle. His hair, like the duke's and Will's, glistened as brightly as newly minted gold. His dark, hooded eyes were wide apart. His shoulders broad. Indeed everything about Carlyle would make most women swoon.

Why, like I did with the nosegay, do I distrust what I see? Yet in one glance I knew Will's heart and soul.

The lively jig followed, and knowing her duty, she smiled and followed as best as she could. Breathing heavier after expertly executing several small leaps, Carlyle led her back to where Alice and Tom waited.

"I believe it is time to return to the castle," he declared.

Exhausted from pretending to enjoy herself without Will, Elizabeth nodded and pulled Alice to her side. As before, the men paced behind them.

They had passed the lace stall when Elizabeth felt a tug on her gown and, looking down, saw an old man with a winking green stone in one ear. He flashed her a gold-toothed smile.

"I know your fortune, my lady. Let me tell it to you." His tent, its flap open, lay behind him.

Instinct made her stop. "Yes, I believe I shall let you tell me the future."

Carlyle lifted one eyebrow. "By all means, amuse yourself. We shall wait here."

"Oh, no, I won't. I'm going in with her." Alice followed closely behind as the gypsy lead Elizabeth away.

Once inside the tent, the man dropped the flap, cutting off the fair sounds. Elizabeth crossed on rag rugs covering the ground to an unsteady-looking chair beside a small table. The air was stuffy and carried the faint smell of garlic.

The gypsy seated himself across from her. "Give me your hand, my lady."

Palm up, she placed her right hand before him on the black, cloth-covered table.

Smiling, his gold teeth gleaming in the candlelight, he looked down.

His expression abruptly changed.

"Don't sit there with your mouth hanging open and your eyes bugging out of your skull. Say something. What do you see?" Alice demanded to know.

"Life. Death." The gypsy jumped up so quickly his chair toppled over. "No more."

"I could have done a better job of it and I don't have the eye." Alice snorted.

I saw his eyes and they were full of terror for me.

Elizabeth rose, took a coin from the small silk purse at her wrist, and placed it on the table.

"Don't give this charlatan a penny!" Alice lunged for

the table but the gypsy was quicker, snatching the coin and backing deeper into the shadows of the tent.

"Great danger," he whispered.

The sounds of the fair returned and an instant later they were gone.

Still seething in indignation, Alice stared after him. "Man had an escape route in the back. No doubt to save himself from dissatisfied customers."

Elizabeth grabbed her arm to look steadily into her eyes. "Promise you will say nothing of this."

Lips pressed in a tight line, Alice nodded.

Emerging from the tent, they found Carlyle looking bored and Tom with an expectant gleam in his wide eyes.

"No, there will be no telling our secrets to you." Alice laughed up at him.

Once again Elizabeth took Alice's arm so they could walk side by side and hoped her dear friend would not have a bruise from the pressure of her fingers.

Reaching the castle, Elizabeth forced herself to move and act normally and not betray the growing unease she felt all around her.

Great danger from where? From whom?

At last they reached her chamber door and she quickly turned to bid Carlyle a good night.

He clasped her hand, carrying it to his lips. "Rest tonight and tomorrow. You are pale. A ride in the brisk air will return the roses to your cheeks. Ride with me the day after."

Knowing she must chart an honorable course for all of them out of this torment, she nodded. "Yes, Carlyle, I shall ride with you."

Once Tom reported the fairgoers had arrived safely back in the castle, Will walked to his father's chambers.

As he did every night, the duke sat in his large carved chair before the fire and waited for him.

Tonight, Will knew, would be different than all others before.

He took a stance in front of the fire, much as his father had done earlier.

The duke lifted his eyes to meet Will's steady gaze. "Tell me."

"I love Elizabeth. I want her for myself."

The shock of saying aloud what was in his heart and soul instead of what he had intended to ask, caused him to grip the mantle, his fingers turning white.

"Do you plan to take her up before you on your horse and flee to Europe? Sell your sword to kings and princes for coin? Disgraced, neither of you would be received by any but the lowest among us. I wonder if you will think of those you leave behind. The men, women, and children who will suffer and perhaps die because you put them in harm's way without the protection and prosperity of alliances made between leaders. Can such love flourish in soil tainted by your selfishness and dishonor?"

Stunned by such words spoken in disdain by his father, Will straightened in boiling anger and disbelief. "Are these the words *your* father used when he convinced you to betray and desert my mother?"

Watching his father's face crumple felt like a kick to his chest, taking away his power to breathe.

In two steps he was in front of his father and fell on one knee. "I was seized by madness. I came to ask permission to gather a troop of men to inspect and fortify our borders. To leave to preserve my honor, not to bring you this pain. Forgive me."

"How can I forgive when I have never forgiven myself?" With trembling fingers, he gripped Will's shoulder. In the firelight the tears drifting down his face sparkled, starkly revealing his pain. "I would give you my heart to feast upon if it could change the past. I know well the love you feel and the agony of your choices."

"Is it right that we must make such choices for others? Should they not be free to make their own?" Will asked quietly, his chest tight with regret.

"In another time, another place, such ideas may flourish and bear fruit. This is our time and our place." The duke rose and Will followed. He looked into cornflower-blue eyes so much like his own. "Out of my love I grant you free choice, Will, to do what your honor dictates and your heart can bear. Whatever you choose, I vow I shall do everything in my power to protect you and Elizabeth from all who might harm you. And I pledge I shall try to make amends to Wharton Keep to protect the peace between us."

Knowing his father spoke the truth, the only decision Will could make settled into his soul.

After Alice, still laughing and reliving her dance with Tom, retired, Elizabeth lay wide-eyed, haunted by waking nightmares.

Her body, awakened to its needs by Will's touch, ached for him. She craved his strength. Wanted to bask in the security his arms offered.

Together we are invincible.

The thought came from deep inside her. From the place she was only beginning to know and still did not fully understand.

She rose and padded to the chest where the celestial girdle slept.

Holding it, running her fingertips over the jewels, the golden crescents of the waxing moon, she sought answers to the questions plaguing her.

Yes, she knew there was great danger, for she felt the energy of darkness around her.

From where does it come? And what should I do to overcome it?

These were the questions which haunted her. Yet they faded, becoming nothing compared to the heart of her torment.

How can I change the course of my life to intersect with Will's?

Feeling the chill of the hours past midnight, she crawled into bed, clasping the jeweled girdle to her breasts, praying its magic would give her the answers.

Alice found her there in the morning.

"God in heaven, you could have hurt yourself with that thing in your bed while you slept!"

Having been granted no answers, but rather a sleepless night, Elizabeth sat weakly on the side of the bed while Alice fussed about, gathering scented water and all Cybil's potions to better help her greet the day.

The knock came at the door as Alice finished lacing Elizabeth's morning robe.

Will, neatly dressed, his hair darkened by water and his skin glowing, stood in the entry.

My prayers have been answered.

Joy exploded through her blood, evaporating her listlessness, propelling her into movement.

"Alice, leave us, please." Surprisingly, she vanished without comment.

Slowly closing the door, Will turned to her.

Not able to wait another moment, she ran to be in the cherished warmth of his arms.

He stood quite still, his hands gripped behind his back.

She swayed to a stop, her eyes searching his closed face. "What has happened?"

"Lady Elizabeth, I have come to tell you I am leaving tomorrow with a troop of my men to fortify our border with Scotland. This will be our last meeting. When I return you shall be my brother's wife."

The words reached her, but she couldn't understand their meaning, so foreign was his face and voice.

When finally they penetrated her confusion she recoiled in disbelief.

"So we are to repeat your mother and father's tragedy."

For an instant she marveled at how she had known what weapon to use to drain his skin of color and bring blue fire to his eyes. To bring life to the hard-controlled muscles of his face.

I know because I am his soul mate.

"Elizabeth, you must understand I can offer you nothing but dishonor."

She held back the tears, the need to throw herself into his arms, pleading with him not to leave her alone. "You can offer me love, can you not, Will?" she asked softly.

His eyes caressed her, giving her the courage to take a step closer.

"Until the end of time, Elizabeth, I shall love you."

"Then do not throw away our future with both hands. I shall find a way for us to be together. I promise."

"At the expense of others? The guilt would destroy both of us." The harsh weariness in his voice stopped her. She sensed his decision had been hard-won, but he had chosen honor, duty.

She would not tell him of the danger she felt gathering around her. She sensed the burden of his choice was nearly more than he could bear. From deep inside, her love for him gave her the strength to meet the open plea in his eyes.

"For now I give you leave to go, Will. Yet I promise this is not the end for us."

She thought he would touch her, willed him to do so, but she saw his shoulders stiffen in resolve. Recognized the determination in the firm set of his jaw. Ached at the agony in his eyes.

Only after the door closed behind him, did she sink to the floor, bury her face in her palms, and weep for what lay ahead for them both.

Dunham Castle, 1601

A dark energy grows heavily around me and I struggle to understand from whence it comes. I alone must discover the source of the danger. I call on the knowledge and power within me which grows daily. From it, I gain strength to accept my need for Will to be by my side for all time and to uncover the path of honor for both of us.

Will believes he must choose honor and duty over our love, and I know I must be patient with his decision until the moment is right to reveal my choice.

I defy the choice my father made for me and plot how I shall fall at his feet and beg him to understand I must be free to seize my own destiny. Out of his love for me I pray he will understand my change of heart. I came here to do my duty and in doing so I have found my heart's desire for all time.

In this time and place I choose both love and honor, for neither can exist without the other. I know my choice will shape your destiny.

Chapter Six

Elizabeth lay awake throughout the long night, counting the hours until Will would leave her.

Eyes acid-dry from endless weeping, she watched Alice leave the chamber to bid farewell to Tom before Will led his troops from the castle. She chose to be spared the torment of that sight for she feared watching him ride away would break even her iron resolve to find an honorable way for them to be together. If she broke, she would fall to her knees, begging him to stay.

I cannot burden him with my need until I forge an honorable path for us both to follow.

Sure in the knowledge that she would find the way and that Will would return to her, she strengthened her resolve to bide her time until all could be as she desired.

"They are safely away?" she asked as Alice entered the room.

"Aye." Her usual smile wavered and then was gone.

"Sorry to see Tom go. Thinking I might stay for a bit after your wedding to see him return."

Icy shivers consumed Elizabeth anew as she thought of her upcoming wedding and what she must do to prevent it. She rose, hurrying to the hot, scented water Alice had brought. "You know you may stay as long as you wish."

"Aye, I know. Miss my bossy sister Jane and Granny Cybil. I'll be full of tales to tell about this fine court and your grand wedding." Laying out Elizabeth's clothes for riding with Carlyle, Alice slid her a worried look. "Speaking of your groom, you don't seem that excited about becoming his countess."

Swirling to face her, Elizabeth forced a smile. "And you say you don't have the eye like your Granny Cybil. No, I do not know Carlyle, nor am I sure I shall like to be his bride, but I shall try to appear more pleasant to not hurt his feelings."

Sensible Alice straightened and stared at her in disbelief. "Elizabeth, what can be done but to do what your father wishes?"

Her heart felt as if it would burst through her bones and skin. She held Alice's hands and squeezed. "I do not yet know. Perhaps a ride in the crisp, fresh air will help clear my head and show me the way."

Hours later, her words to Alice haunted Elizabeth as Carlyle kissed her wrist before helping her mount her horse. As always, his touch sent shivers of fear along her skin and into her heart.

It is not his doing that my heart belongs to another and his touch repulses me. I must be kind. I do not wish to hurt him.

He led her in a new direction, foreign to her. As they

rode, she saw no small, neat farms, or hailed any of the scouts who guarded the duke's lands. Where Carlyle led there was only forest and a strange stillness.

Smiling, she pretended to be interested in his talk of hawking and hunting. His pleasant companionship, the air cool and fresh on her face, her love of riding, could not quench her strange unease. She had the oddest feeling that she was being led somewhere she would not like to reach.

She kept glancing behind her, hoping to see a familiar rider, a beloved face. Someone who would stay by her side, to make her feel safe on this strange ride into a part of the forest she had not visited.

Will! Will, if only you were by my side.

Her heart sent the plea while her mind tried to stop wishing for it to be true.

I must make my desire to have Will always by my side come to pass. I must refuse to marry Carlyle, a man who I do not love, and in truth, fear.

The knowledge of what she must do echoed again and again in her head as she rode beside him, deeper into thicker brush and tall trees which blocked the sun.

"I want to take you to my special place, Elizabeth."

Instinct made her hesitate. Duty and a certain guilt at what she planned demanded she nod in agreement.

As they rode into the sun, his men and the supply horses laden with food, casks of beer, helmets, steel plates, spearheads, and swords at his back, Will laid out to his lieutenant all his plans to fortify the duke's border with Scotland and to secure the newly acquired lands to the east.

The lands Elizabeth will bring to her marriage to Carlyle.

In the cold hours before dawn, Will had paced the courtyard, hoping and dreading she might appear to bid him farewell. Leaning heavily upon the duke's strong arm and Will's grandfather while holding Stephen, Laurel had sent him off with tears, embraces, and prayers for a safe and swift return.

His gut clenched again, remembering Alice running into the torch-lit courtyard, believing for one glorious moment that Elizabeth had followed and he could see her one last time. He felt again the aching disappointment when he realized Alice was alone, coming to say good-bye to his smitten lieutenant.

Now, face solemn, Tom rode beside him, Alice's parcel of ginger and other concoctions she swore would keep him healthy tucked securely in his saddlebag.

Although Tom had appeared to listen and grasp Will's plans for the weeks of their campaign, his unusually grim countenance told another story.

"We shall return before you are forgotten. Stop fretting," Will coaxed and was rewarded by a grin.

"Aye, Alice is quite a girl. I hope she stays a bit after the grand wedding."

The grand wedding of my brother to the woman I love.

Images burned through his mind and seared his heart.

Carlyle's hands touching the warmth of Elizabeth's lush, responsive body. Carlyle pushing his fingers through the glory of her hair, pulling her close to plunder the sweetness of her lips. Carlyle possessing her.

Pounding jealousy and fear shattered all other feelings,

leaving only one at his center. She had asked what might be greater than honor. He had always known the answer but been fearful of accepting the truth.

Will! She was calling to him as he had called to her in the courtyard. He could *see* her being led into a secluded glade by Carlyle. Her fear poured through him, drowning his iron resolve. He must make sure she was safe.

No longer able to still his deep-seated fear for her, he held up his arm and his troops halted behind him. "Tom, take the men back to Dunham Castle. I shall meet you there."

Wheeling his horse, he raced to find her before it was too late.

Patches of sunshine, falling down through the arch of trees above them, played across Carlyle's intense face as he led Elizabeth into a quiet glade. Thick, low bushes surrounded an odd circle of flat grass. In one corner a small pool was fed by an underground spring. She slid off her horse, allowing it to drink there.

Her defenses weakened by fatigue, she couldn't step away before Carlyle clasped her hand, pressing his lips to her birthmark.

"I have chosen you for this. And for this." With his fingertips he stroked the celestial girdle around her hips.

His touch and smile froze her with unease and the edge of fear she didn't understand.

"Your birthmark and girdle represent the old arts of which I know much. As do you, my beautiful Elizabeth. Here, I brought you to my special place to show you who I am and what we shall be together."

He reached into what appeared to be a hollow between felled logs and pulled out a heavy, black-hooded robe.

Every instinct screamed danger and she backed away one step.

He placed it around his shoulders before he pushed aside the thick brush. There stood a stone altar stained with blood such as Cybil, had described to her as the worship place of the dark ways.

Sickened, now realizing why she had instinctively feared Carlyle, Elizabeth retreated even farther from him. "You practice the dark magic."

His eyes wide and flickering with emotions which froze Elizabeth, Carlyle, smiling, moved closer to her. "Ah, Elizabeth, you are a child of such magic. Marked by the pagan gods. Within you lives both darkness and light. It is the purity of your heart which shields you from all you are destined to be. When you are joined with me, I shall release your full dark power. Together we shall conquer time and space."

"Never!" Rage and defiance swelled in her breast, and she pulled the hidden golden dagger from her celestial girdle and aimed it at his heart.

Carlyle laughed. "Good. You like your play rough, Elizabeth. As do I."

He lunged toward her.

Some force within her, like unseen hands, flung him back away from her.

His triumphant face turned her blood to ice. "You are more than I had hoped. By our wedding day I will have the measure of your magic and match it."

Frozen in disbelief and terror, she couldn't move until her birthmark began to tingle, warming her body, giving her the strength and knowledge to defy him. "You do not match me this day, my lord."

Eyes wide, laughing, he again moved toward her. "My bewitching Elizabeth, it is heedless to struggle. The old gods have decreed this the time and place where we shall join our powers."

The force of her revulsion flung him to the ground. "I believe the gods have decreed this the time and place for me to discover your darkness and reject it."

His face a mask of disbelief and rage, he leapt to his feet. "You shall not defy me!"

On its own power, her golden dagger left her fingers to hover at his exposed throat. She sucked air into her hot lungs in awe at the power she felt coursing through her and with the dagger as if it was a part of her. "Leave now, Carlyle, or I shall destroy you. I swear it."

Laughing, he ripped off his robe, hid it once more, and leaped upon his horse. "Follow the setting sun back to Dunham Castle and ponder what we will soon be together. For I swear it shall come to pass. There is naught you can do to defy the old gods. You cannot flee from this destiny. Even if you try, you shall fail."

Fearing he spoke the truth and, weakened by despair and horror, she fell to her knees as she returned the dagger to its place in her girdle.

I shall never be a creature of darkness with him. Never. Never. Never.

Hearing the sound of an approaching rider, fearing Carlyle might be returning, she swayed to her feet, ready to pull the dagger free once again.

Will slid off his horse and ran rapidly across the glade to her. "Elizabeth! Love, I am here."

Her relief was white-hot, scalding, a blaze too bright to bear.

Instinct, hunger, desire long denied and now free drove her hands into the hair at the nape of his neck, bringing his face, his lips so close.

Every reservation gone, Will pulled her even closer, parting her lips, tasting her. His mouth stroked over hers again and again as he dragged her tight against his body. She breathed in his heat and his scent, craving more.

In burning desire, in full acceptance of what she wanted, she twisted into his body, throwing back her head, exposing her throat and breasts to his searching kisses.

His hands ran up and down her spine, sending shuddering thrills along her tingling nerves.

"If Carlyle hurt you, I shall kill him!" His voice sounded hoarse.

Afraid, she held him tighter. "Leave him! He did not harm me, though he's revealed himself to be a monster." She cupped his face with her palms. Every cell in her body burned for him and against these feelings duty faded to nothing. "Only you have the power to hurt me, Will."

Laying his forehead softly against hers, he lifted his hands to stroke her face. "Forgive me, Elizabeth. I was wrong. I can never let you go. Ever."

"Nor I you. I pray that out of love my father will release me from my pledge to marry Carlyle and I will beg him on my knees to bless our union with a dowry. As I pray the duke's love for you shall sustain us," she whispered and kissed him deeply and tenderly with an intensity which left her weak. "Please take me somewhere safe. Away from this evil place. Where we can be together as we are meant to be."

Will hesitated, his heart pounding against her breasts.

She saw the decision in his eyes before, at last, he nodded. "My grandfather's cottage. He keeps my old room ready for me."

Elizabeth clung to Will, resting her cheek against his shoulder, as he cradled her in his arms before him on his horse.

Leading her stallion, they galloped into the courtyard of a large cottage at the edge of deep woods.

Purple twilight surrounded them as Will's grandfather, dressed in a knee-length cloak for traveling, hurried across the cobblestones toward them. "Will, you have returned. What has happened?"

"Crucial matters here have brought me home. I found Lady Elizabeth faint from fatigue while riding. It was closer to bring her here, Grandfather."

He peered up into both their faces. "I understand. I shall tell the duke and duchess that Elizabeth should remain here for the night. They need send no servants. My own shall attend her."

"Tell Stephen's nursemaid I, too, shall return on the morrow." She felt Will's arm tighten around her like armor.

She turned her head and unflinchingly met his grandfather's stare, as she bared her love for Will openly.

He nodded. "Then it shall be as it should be."

• • •

There was little Will had not seen in court, the battlefield, or the bedroom, yet watching Elizabeth walk to the warm, spring-fed pool at the edge of the woods behind his grandfather's cottage filled him with wonder.

He slipped his arm around her waist and her head rested on his shoulder. Freed of her ribbons, her ebony hair blown by the evening winds flowed across his throat and chest, filling the air he breathed with the scent of lavender.

At the far side of the pool they came to the limestone rim, which was festooned with vines and heavy purple blossoms.

Laughing, she slipped off her kid boots, slowly uncoiled her celestial girdle and placed it carefully on the ground. Wearing only her loose gown with hanging sleeves, she walked into the shallows.

Turning back to him, her thick, wavy hair cascading over her breasts, her huge eyes lit by the setting sun, she beckoned to him.

"Come, Will. Join me in paradise."

Leaving most of his clothes in a pile next to hers, Will waded toward her. He felt the warm spring water rush over his feet and calves.

To him, Elizabeth was a creature of magic, of desire, of love he would follow through eternity.

She arched her back gracefully over his arm and he twirled her around, the water tugging at the fabric of her gown.

Closing her eyes, she smiled. "My old nurse, Cybil, taught me to always submerge my body in life-giving water."

They held one another in a wet embrace, his desire matched by hers.

"My grandfather taught me the same." With one movement he drew her from the pool and carried her to the flat, wide limestone shelf.

Her gown, heavy with spring water, clung to her. Slowly his eyes traveled over her body to rest on her wide gaze. "You are the giver of life, Elizabeth. For me. Always. I know this is our destiny."

Elizabeth pulled him closer until she was inside his embrace, her lips open to the heavy strokes of his tongue.

Ancient wisdom guided her to strip him of his garments, his body beautiful in the light of the waxing moon. Blood spinning through her veins, she felt like a new creature.

He slid his palms along her spine, curled his fingers over her shoulders, and freed her gown so that it fell to her hips.

She felt no embarrassment, no instinct to cover herself. Instead she pushed her gown down her body and over her ankles to pool on the smooth, cool stone.

She wanted to be as naked as Will. She wanted no scrap of clothing, *nothing*, between them.

She felt the beating of his heart as her heavy breasts moved against his warm, damp chest. His fingers fanned across her delicate skin, lifting her breasts, his thumbs brushing gently across her nipples. A sweet throbbing began deep inside her. He moved from nipple to nipple, sucking each deeply into his mouth. The pleasure drove her to feverishly whisper his name over and over.

"Yes, love. I know. I want to bring you even greater pleasure." He nuzzled her throat with his warm lips and moved down her quivering stomach, leaving a trail of fire. She gloried in the sensation that was like a carillon ringing through her. She arched to press closer to him, her thighs restless and hot beneath his kisses.

He cradled her hips and then so very slowly he slipped two fingers inside her. She sobbed once and felt the pattern of his breathing change to meet hers.

Holding her gently, he eased her thighs apart on the cool stones. "Elizabeth, I want to be a part of you," he whispered.

He entered her slowly, filling her completely, and becoming a part of her forever.

The fit of their bodies was exquisite.

Fever racked her body as they moved to a primal rhythm from the beginning of time. It was soul meeting soul in a blinding radiance, leaving his image imprinted on her forever.

Elizabeth fell asleep while their bodies were still tangled together. Will tried to rouse her with whispers into the sweet shell of her ear.

"You have imprinted your soul on mine, Elizabeth. For eternity."

Her fragrant hair tickled his face as he dragged slow kisses down her nose to her parted lips.

"Yes. As you have on mine. It is our destiny." She sighed, her eyes still heavy with sensual fatigue.

Folding her into his arms, he felt again the need to protect her. "Come with me to a safe haven."

They left their clothes spread to dry across the limestone and walked naked, save for the golden girdle coiled around Elizabeth's beautiful hips, to the back door of the cottage.

Will led her up the narrow steps to his room. There he

slowly removed the jeweled girdle from her warm flesh and laid her gently back on the pillows.

"Rest, love. Tomorrow will be a new day for us."

He climbed in bed beside her and they curved together as if they were one. Elizabeth in his arms, her hair ebony silk across his chest, her breath warm on his throat, Will felt complete.

Is this what my parents felt together? Like they were one? How could they live without this? Without one another?

Fear torched through him like a blaze destroying all in its path.

Elizabeth is betrothed to my brother. This new day must bring an end to that. Together, Elizabeth and I shall forge a new beginning with honor.

Smiling, he watched Elizabeth curl onto her side, her palms together as if in prayer. Unable to resist, he pressed a kiss upon her slightly parted lips before leaving her.

Dawn had barely lit the sky when he found his grandfather beside his forge. Will saw that he had found their clothes and brought them near the fire to dry.

"I have been waiting for you, Will. Hold out your hand to me."

Not understanding, but obeying nonetheless, Will held out his hand and his grandfather placed two warm rings of gold on his flat palm.

"Read the inscriptions, Will."

He lifted the smaller ring, reading it in the flickering light of the flames. "Doubt the stars are fire." Then he slowly rotated the larger ring in the glow of firelight. "Yet never doubt my love." He placed the rings together and saw that stars encircled the word love and on Elizabeth's ring the crescent moon was slightly raised. He realized it mirrored the waxing moons on her celestial girdle. Mirrored the one above them last night when they had made love.

"I saw this day coming, Will. I have used a special combination of elements with a strand of your hair from when you were a babe and silken strands of Elizabeth's from the night she watched over Laurel. These rings will last for eternity if your love is true. When joined, they will produce an unconquerable power. Are you prepared to face the future with Elizabeth?"

Will took a long, silent breath of flame-tinged warm air. "I want eternity with her. We can forge it with the love and support of you and my father. Our choices are made, we shall have no other love."

Charles Grey's Cottage, England, 1601

This day set our path for eternity. We reached this firmament through valleys of despair and danger.

Will believes his honor demands he leave me to marry his brother.

I learned the fear I felt with Carlyle is real and his evil runs deeper than anyone knows.

He is a creature of the dark magic. How powerful I have yet to discover.

Yet I know nothing is powerful enough to keep Will and me apart.

I wait for him here in this bed still warm from his body, his scent perfuming my flesh.

I wait for his touch, his kiss, our bodies and souls to become one.

I wait for him to return to the sweet, safe haven of my arms.

My choice is made, and there shall be no other.

Chapter Seven

Carlyle's fiery rage drove him from the dying embers of the fireplace to the door of his dark chamber again and again. At last he heard Florea's shuffling footsteps. With deliberate care, he lit two torches, holding them up to further heat his flushed face.

Flinging her palms out in front of her eyes, she fell back one step. "What has happened to anger you so?"

"You lied to me, old woman." His breath hissed between his clenched teeth. "I did as you commanded. I showed Elizabeth my altar. Told her what we shall be together and her magic flung me away. Rejected me! Not embraced me as you promised!"

Her milky eyes narrowed. "I tell you, the old gods have spoken to me. You are the chosen one who shall release Elizabeth's powers. You know well the way is not always clear. You must make the proper sacrifice to the old gods to show you the future. I have taught you how it must be done, have I not?"

Mollified, knowing she had showed him paths to power others could never understand or would be too fearful to follow, he blew out the candles, plunging them into welcome darkness.

"So be it. Tomorrow it shall be done. Then at last I will take what is rightfully mine."

In the quiet light of dawn, Will entered his old room, swiftly shed his clothes, and sat beside Elizabeth on the bed. He found the underside of her chin and with gentle fingers tilted her face up toward his.

The faint shine of her eyes, like emeralds, took his breath away. He found the power to draw air into his lungs once more and smiled.

"Wake, love, to a new day."

He rose to his knees on the bed and she joined him, her naked beauty unearthly in the frosty light of the warm room.

He took her hand, carrying it to his lips, before he slipped the ring upon her finger. "Doubt the stars are fire, Elizabeth," he whispered.

Her eyes widened and she took the second ring from his outstretched palm. She glanced at it for two heartbeats before lifting his hand to her lips and placing the ring upon his finger.

"Yet never doubt my love, Will." Emotion scratched her voice.

His need for her flamed through him. "Come to me in love."

Will's face softened in a longing Elizabeth felt low in her body. Her heart seemed to stop, then start once more, the tightness in her throat spreading down to her breasts.

She wanted him to touch her and said the words aloud. "I love you touching me in love, Will. Please never cease until the end of time."

His hands moved down her back to cup her hips and press her to his, sending shivers through her.

"Open yourself to me," he murmured against her quivering lips.

Dizzy with pleasure, she would have collapsed had he not caught her to press her down among the pillows and covers.

"Lie with me forever, Elizabeth."

His whispers of love warmed her throat and her breasts, his mouth soothing the throbbing ache there. Her flesh grew hot under his touch.

She arched herself into him, wanting his hands and mouth to feed the need growing within her.

With shaking hands, she cupped his face with her fingers to gaze into his eyes. "I want this for eternity and beyond."

He kissed every part of her and she neither knew nor cared about naught but this hot, wet ecstasy.

She wrapped her legs around his body and held him tight, feeling his deep shudders each time he thrust inside her. At a moment suspended between exquisite pleasure and pain, her release matched his and she wept for joy, feeling cherished in his arms.

Will was so beautiful lying beside her, his skin alive with fresh color, his eyes watching her.

"Wait for me here. I shall return and together we will go

to the duke to declare our love before him. Honor demands that I first speak to my brother."

Fear surged through her. She flung herself onto his chest to stop him. "No! Do not go! You know Carlyle has become a creature of darkness."

He soothed her with a kiss on her brow. "Yet he is still my blood. Do you trust me?"

"With my soul. Always," she whispered, an ache at the back of her throat.

"Then I promise we shall have nights like this through eternity. Wait for me, love. I will return to you."

Carlyle rode into the quiet glade and, leaving his horse tethered, quickly retrieved his robe and jeweled dagger from their hiding place.

The cold air felt heavy today as if a storm might brew, yet the sky remained cloudless. The bright sun showed him his snare held a struggling prize.

The hare was fat, its fur thick. A worthy sacrifice to the gods.

Chanting the incarnations to the old, dark practices taught to him by Florea, with one hand he held the frightened, fighting animal high above the altar.

"You shall show me the future," he cried and plunged the jeweled dagger deep into the hare's beating heart.

He opened his fingers, knowing the way the sacrifice's limbs fell upon the stone altar and the direction the blood spurted and flowed would reveal what was to come.

What he saw took his breath away. For one heartbeat,

a crumbling remnant of regret and fear for what he must do stirred deep within him. Acceptance of what this would bring to him extinguished all other feelings save triumph. He sucked blood-perfumed air into his lungs and smiled.

Will carried the image of Elizabeth in his heart and mind as he rode back to the glade where he'd known Carlyle would be with her yesterday.

He smelled the blood before he saw his brother's hooded figure holding a jeweled dagger and the rabbit sacrificed upon the altar.

Sickened by what his brother had become, Will ran quickly to grab his shoulder, twisting him around. Carlyle's eyes were wild with a look Will had never seen before and his lips were smeared with the rabbit's blood.

"This is madness!" Will flung his brother away in disgust.

Carlyle pushed back the hood and, smiling, lifted his fingers to spread the blood over his face.

"It is the old magic of the gods, Will. Its power shall soon be known by all."

Will's hand rested on his sword. "Never will I allow this darkness to touch Elizabeth or any who I love. Nor will I repeat the mistake of the past." He stared into his brother's eyes. "Out of the love we once shared I have come to tell you Elizabeth is mine. Our love is true and everlasting. I will go to our father to ask for your betrothal to be severed and gain permission to marry Elizabeth."

Carlyle's heavy shoulders tensed and his breath hissed. "Always the favorite son asking our father for more bounty.

No doubt he will grant you all you desire."

"I pray it be true." Regret sliced through him, for in the depths of Carlyle's mad eyes he had glimpsed a glimmer of pain. Despite his loyalty to his blood, Will wanted to be away from this place of darkness. Away from the evil he had tried to deny in his brother.

"Save yourself and end this," Will pleaded and turned away.

"I shall. For now I know what is to be done," Carlyle laughed.

Excruciating, white-hot pain exploded in Will's back, dropping him to his knees. Shock rendered him sluggish, and he struggled against the nausea rising in his throat. Knowing to survive he must defend himself, he pushed to his feet.

A blinding kick to his head knocked him to his side.

Looking up through a red haze of agony, he saw Carlyle standing over him, his bloodied dagger in his fist.

Rage, disbelief, and the desperate need to return to Elizabeth gave him the strength to rise to fight his brother for his life.

Snarling, Carlyle kicked him in the gut, and the violence of the blow exploded such pain through his body that Will fell back, struggling to draw air in his lungs with his brother's spurred boot pressing hard into his chest.

Smiling, Carlyle knelt and ripped the Posey ring from his finger. "I know what magic this represents. I will cast this ring into the darkest deepest pit of the sea. Powerless, there it will rest in its watery grave forever. As you will lie eaten by worms in your earthly grave for eternity."

Tasting blood in his mouth, feeling life draining from his body, Will summoned the strength to spit in his brother's face. "It matters not what evil you do," he gasped, pain all he knew. "Elizabeth shall never be yours. Now. Or ever. Our love will endure beyond this life."

Carlyle leaned closer and Will saw the madness in his eyes.

"Fool! My magic will always be more powerful than eternal love." Carlyle frowned, his eyes suddenly those of the young brother Will had known. "Ah, brother, you look pale and in such pain. I loved you once when we were boys. Before I realized the truth. To honor that, I shall be merciful."

He flicked the tip of his dagger across Will's wrist, the sting short and sharp, the blood warm dripping into his cupped palm.

"Yes, Will, you will die quickly now. And I shall be the one to soothe your loved ones. Think on that in your last moments of life."

His words gave Will a rush of adrenaline to roll over, to try to rise, to refuse to give in to the agony ripping his body apart.

Laughing, Carlyle moved aside thick branches, shed his robe in their small dark cave, and mounted his horse.

He pranced to where Will, fighting with all his draining power, had risen to one knee. "Stop struggling, brother. It is your destiny to die here this day."

Will watched him ride away through a thickening darkness in his eyes and an icy chill shuddering through his body. Gathering the last of his strength, Will called to the winds. "Elizabeth, come to me."

• • • •

Charles Grey's Cottage, England, 1601

In these last hours I have discovered where the sun is born.

His image is drawn on my soul, and he is imprinted upon my heart.

It is Will's smile. Will's touch. Will's kiss.

We have become one in all ways.

We have pledged our love with Posey rings which will last for eternity. And so we will confess to the duke, who I know will bless our love.

In joy I have made my choice.

Yet in this moment, my joy is turning to fear. Is it because I know Will, out of honor, has gone to Carlyle?

The winds call to me and I hear…

"Will!" she screamed, dropping her pen.

Terror a living force consuming her, Elizabeth heard Will calling for her to come to him.

Trembling, she fumbled to dress in a loose gown and coiled her girdle around her as she stumbled down the narrow steps of the cottage.

In the courtyard, Charles Grey looked up from mounting his horse. "Elizabeth, what is wrong, child?"

"It is Will! I must reach him in time!" she cried.

He tried to stop her but she wrenched free, grabbing the reins and leaping upon the horse. "He is at the secluded glade. Follow me."

Fear squeezing like a vise upon all her senses, her blood running cold, she galloped over the fields to the place where Will had found her.

Her frigid blood froze her in horror, seeing him on the flat grass, his blood soaking red the earth beneath him.

In her need to reach him, she half fell from her horse,

scrabbled to her feet, stumbled toward him to sink to her knees at his side. "Will, I am here. Love, I am here."

Slowly his eyes opened and she saw a flame flicker in their depths. "I knew you would come." His breath, shallow and low, filled her with terror.

"Yes, love. Always. I shall save you. I promise." Tears nearly blinding her, she pressed a jeweled crescent from the girdle against his wrist. As before, the wound closed into a moon-shaped scar. "I can heal you with my magic," she sobbed, pressing the crescent moon against the stab wound in his back.

Her breath caught in horror.

It is not healing.

In roiling, scalding desperation, she pressed another crescent against the wound and another and another, held each tighter, held each longer, yet still Will's blood bubbled around her hands and into the earth.

Her moans of anguish were carried by the wind, rustling the leaves above her.

"It is too deep, too deep," she sobbed, cradling him in her arms, rocking him as her tears wet his face and hair.

"Elizabeth, my love. Must…overcome…Carlyle's magic," he gasped, his breathing more labored, the flame flickering in his eyes.

Through her dark agony arose a great swell of strength, and a shuddering understanding of her power washed over her.

"We shall overcome Carlyle." She kissed Will's cold lips, trying to warm them. "Love, do not fear this darkness, for it is but a moment. This is not the end for us, my love. I know I carry your child and I promise Stephen will be granted his birthright. For us, heaven can wait. If it takes a thousand lifetimes, we will be together again."

"I believe you...Elizabeth..." His eyes drifted shut and she pressed her lips to his to feel and taste his last breath.

She flung back her head, crying out her rage. Dark clouds rolled across the sun above her. Jagged shafts of light cut the blackness and the heavens roared.

Beneath her, the earth trembled before she heard the horses galloping toward them.

Cradling Will in her arms, she looked up into his grandfather's face.

Aging before her eyes, Charles Grey knelt beside her, Will's soldiers at his back.

Sick to her soul, yet full of primal knowledge of what she must do to secure the future for all of them, she lied. "It was the thieves who roam these woods who did this deed."

Raindrops mingled with his tears as Will's grandfather nodded. "Come, child, we must take Will home to Dunham Castle."

Tom, frank tears and anguish stark upon his face, lifted Will into his arms, carrying him to his horse.

"No!" Elizabeth screamed, not wanting to relinquish her love.

Charles Grey, his eyes steady and full of knowledge met hers. "Will is gone, Elizabeth." His arms surprisingly strong, he held her back. "You must let his bodily remains be put to rest."

Trembling, her world a storm of vengeance and disbelief, she fell to her knees, weeping.

"Elizabeth, remember what Will would wish you to do." The challenge in his grandfather's voice snapped her back to the moment. To what she knew she must do to keep her promises.

With Charles Grey's help, she rose to her feet, and leaning upon him, climbed onto her saddle for the long, agonizing ride home to Dunham Castle.

The heavens opened and a storm of raindrops mingled with her tears and those of Will's men.

Charles Grey had sent a scout ahead with the tragic news. As they slowly entered the strong, high walls of the castle, the bells tolled, and in the courtyard, the duke and Laurel waited.

Elizabeth, wild with grief, searched for Carlyle, her fingers eager on her dagger, ready to pierce his heart.

His face still and blank, he stood beside the duke. Yet she saw that he gave away his fear by rubbing the hilt of his blade with his long fingers.

I cannot destroy him for the sake of my unborn child I sense within me, for my power has told it is true. I must protect Stephen and keep my promises to Will.

Weeping, the duke gently took Will's body into his arms and sank to the cobblestones. "My son. My son," he cried his anguish to the heavens.

Laurel threw herself down beside him, her fine hair a veil over Will's still face, before she collapsed in despair.

From Elizabeth's agony arose a strength she could not have believed possible. Her world lay shattered around her yet she found the courage to rise, to command. *I will not reveal my knowledge to Carlyle until the moment is right for my revenge.*

She nodded to him, standing stiffly over the body of the brother he had slain, before she turned to stare into the duke's grief-stricken eyes. "Will must be taken to the chapel, your Grace," she said gently. Somehow her steadiness and the truth of her words reached him and he nodded. "So be it."

At some point, she realized Alice was beside her. Recognized her bedchamber. Allowed Alice to strip from her the clothes soaked with Will's blood.

Her body performed its duties, yet her mind remained separate, steadying on what she must do to secure the future for those she loved.

Alice, her eyes red-rimmed and as frightened as Elizabeth had ever seen them, studied her. "Can you do it? The duke has sent a servant to escort you to his chambers."

Elizabeth lifted her chin and followed.

Charles Grey was waiting in the warm, softly lit room. He gripped her hands and stared into her eyes, a question in his.

"It is as it was written in our stars," she whispered, trying to believe it herself.

"I accept and understand our destinies." He nodded and closed the door, leaving her alone with the duke.

Eyes wide and wild with grief, tears coursing down his strong face, he paced from door to fire and back again. "This is my punishment. To lose those I love most." He turned to face her. "I know of Will's great love for you. Tell me your free choice and I shall give you my kingdom as I should have given it to Will."

Led by instinct and the power of her promise to Will, she clasped the duke's hands and looked steadily into his dazed eyes.

"I shall be your daughter as Will was your son. The union between the House of Lennox and the House of Wharton will take place. The people will be happy and secure in our alliance."

The duke shook his head in disbelief. "But without Will shall there ever again be joy in our hearts?"

She held her hands over her womb and thought of Stephen. "I swear before God there shall be joy. I vow to show you the way as Will would want me to do."

Dunham Castle, 1601

The heavens weep tears for us and the great winds carry our sorrow across the land.

The court is in mourning, each of us finding our way through this dark torment. In my chamber, feeling Will's child within me, holding his son in my arms, his sweet, soft cheek pressed to my bosom as I relive again and again those final moments with my love in the glade.

Again I feel the terror of finding Will fallen upon the grass, blood gushing from his wounds, staining red the earth beneath him. Again feel my joy when I press a crescent from my celestial girdle against his flesh and it heals into a scar of the waxing moon upon his wrist as it did on Laurel's forehead.

Again the blackness consumes me as the powers of my celestial girdle are not great enough to heal the deep stab wound in Will's back.

My greatest enemy, Carlyle, rubs his fingertips over the jeweled hilt of his dagger, his eyes hooded when he looks at me now. He does not know if his evil deed is secret. If I know he wielded the dagger which killed Will.

Yet I must marry him. In his grief and with my encouragement, the duke has declared the wedding must go forward, the alliance between Wharton Keep and Dunham Castle forged. He says it will give him pleasure to call me daughter even though the ceremony is brief and there will be no merriment.

I will act well my role in this play.

Then when the moment is right I shall step to the edge of the stage between the light and the darkness beyond. From this place, hidden yet exposed, I will claim what is right and just for those I love. It shall be on my wedding night, for then I can secure the future I promised Will.

Chapter Eight

Elizabeth moved through the first week of life without Will in a waking nightmare.

Her wedding day dawned and Alice helped bathe and oil her body as if for a lover. Elizabeth was a lifeless statue, allowing Alice to coil her hair with pearls and choose a gown with a low bodice, so her breasts swelled above the lace ruffle.

As Elizabeth swept from her chamber, Alice stopped her. "You don't need to do this. You can come back to Wharton Keep with me. All would welcome you with open arms."

Saddened to lose her dear friend, her last link to the security of her home, her old life, Elizabeth kissed Alice's warm cheek. "I can't. This is my destiny."

It was as if she stood outside her body, watching the ceremony which made her Carlyle's bride. She felt nothing, heard nothing. The only touchstones of reality were the loss-stricken eyes of the duke, the tortured smile of gentle Laurel, and the knowing eyes of Will's grandfather. Throughout, she did not recoil from Carlyle's touch as every sense demanded in rebellion. Nor did she flinch from his gaze, although the force of her will shuddered in the struggle. As she had planned, Elizabeth acted well the dutiful bride.

Alice gone, Elizabeth dismissed the remaining servants. Alone she awaited her groom in her chambers, which were lit with low candles and a roaring fire.

At a scratch on the door she called, "Enter."

Florea walked slowly into the darkened room.

Elizabeth now knew Florea's true nature. She did not move to help the old nurse's tortured walk across the chamber but remained silent in front of the fire.

"My lady, I come with a small offering." Florea gazed upward into Elizabeth's face as she held out a beautifully embroidered night robe of silver and gold. "Long ago I wove this to be worn by Carlyle's bride on their wedding night. Would you indulge an old woman who has loved Carlyle from his first cry? I have wished for him to possess all that is rightfully his and I know with you it shall be true."

Elizabeth took the robe into her hands. "Yes, with me Carlyle shall receive what is rightfully his due."

She watched Florea shuffle out, having foreseen that within a fortnight the old woman would die of a broken heart, deserted by the one she loved. She would die alone and unmourned as she deserved.

Elizabeth turned, throwing the robe onto the burning logs. She watched as the silver-and-gold threads sparked red before dying into embers.

Carlyle did not knock or ask permission to enter. He walked proudly in long strides to claim his prize. Yet in the chamber's cobweb of shadows and light, she caught the glint of uncertainty in his eyes. Of fear.

In that moment, she stepped out of the shadows to confront him. "Yes, be afraid, Carlyle. For I know you murdered your brother."

His eyes narrowed into slits alive with both fear and vengeance. "Elizabeth, I did only what the old gods decreed. The magic which existed between you and Will was ordained by the gods. It was his destiny to die because of his love for you as it is our destiny to be together. You know I am the one to release your full powers. As I shall do this night."

Rage and grief tore through every fiber of her body as she knew that his words were true. The price of her magic was Will's life. She lifted her chin, and through the agony in her chest, answered him. "Yes, you speak true, Carlyle. Through your abominable cruelty and deceit you have made me recognize and accept my full powers. Powers you shall never possess. This night or any other," she taunted.

His eyes blazed with rage. "Silence, witch! You cannot defeat me and what has been destined to be. The old gods have spoken!" He reached out his hand as if to cover her mouth.

He lunged at her, again and again, and each time Elizabeth's powers pushed him away. Tiring of his hated presence, she waved her hand and Carlyle was flung across the room, crashing against the stone wall, falling, tangled in the tapestry which had covered it.

Gasping, his eyes narrow, he laughed, the sound low and guttural in his throat. "This trick of yours is nothing. My power is becoming greater each day. More than enough to thwart you and your so called great love."

Through the soul-wrenching loss of Will at Carlyle's hand had come the realization of her power. At last she understood the birthright, Cybil, had prophesied. "I foresee that you and I shall duel through time until I defeat you, Carlyle. I know the exact moment you will draw your last breath. And I promise you, I shall be there."

She saw fear and his coward's plan in his eyes and smiled. "Yes, Carlyle, flee from this place, from me, believing it will keep you safe. It shall not."

"We shall see whose power is greater. I'll return when it is time to defeat you, my bewitching Elizabeth," Carlyle promised her, backing from the room.

As her wedding night faded into the new dawn, the wind biting at her skin, she watched from the parapet as Carlyle rode away with his men. Their saddlebags bulged with her dowry and much of the duke's treasury.

Slowly, she walked to Will's chamber and was startled to find Alice, a slumbering Stephen in her arms.

Grinning, Alice rose and carefully gave Stephen into her keeping. "You'll be wanting him, I'm thinking. I sent his nursemaid away and took the liberty of telling her I'd be taking her job."

Weak with surprise and blazing relief, Elizabeth sank into the chair, clasping Stephen to her breasts. "I don't understand. I thought your greatest desire was to return to your family at Wharton Keep."

"Well, I've been thinking you might be needing me." Her snapping brown eyes slid to Stephen and settled on

Elizabeth's womb. "Don't have the eye but I've got eyes in my head. And I've been thinking about destiny. Seems to me Granny Cybil saw Tom was mine. That's why she told me I needed to come with you. Surely that boy's got a bit of the Scots in him with that carroty mop. He needs a good English lass to keep him in line, don't you think?"

The return of joy came with a slight tickle, and she chuckled. "I think Tom is a very lucky man."

"Me, too," Alice said with her usual cheekiness. "I'll leave you alone now, Elizabeth. But I'm here. To stay."

Grateful, she sat rocking Will's son. Once he awoke and blinked up at her with his father's eyes before his lids drifted shut again. Now he slept again upon her breasts.

Hours later, the duke found her there still, holding Stephen.

His face grave, he knelt beside her. "Carlyle has gone, Elizabeth."

She lifted Stephen high in her arms and stood to confront the duke as she had planned. "It matters not that he has fled. Stephen is your rightful heir. Through him live Maude and Will. Through him you shall feel their love. Once again feel joy."

She knew in her heart that the duke did not yet fully realize her words were true for all time.

Very soon the day shall come when you must understand.

He left her then, alone, in the chamber of her lover. The father of the unborn child she cherished within her.

Cradling the sweetly sleeping Stephen on her lap, Elizabeth pressed her lips against her Posey ring.

The forces of nature which she had unleashed gathered around her. Became a part of her. Filled her with primal knowledge, lost and now rediscovered. *Together we are invincible.* She knew it would always be true for through the veil of time she had seen the truth.

I shall find you, Will.

It is written in our stars.

It is our destiny.

Dunham Castle, 1603

From the moment I met Will, I could not see life without him by my side. Now I see the future in the smile of our beautiful daughter, Serena, and in the wide, wise eyes of the son of my heart, Stephen. With them by my side, I do not fear that we are besieged.

Carlyle and his mercenaries are encamped on the plain outside our walls. The duke came to me at dawn but it was not necessary. Rumormongers say there is a woman with him and a boy-child she names his heir.

The duke has aged before my eyes, growing grayer and more lined since our sweet Laurel has grown weaker despite all Charles Grey can do to heal her. I sense his strength of purpose seeping away. The children and I will nurse his invisible wounds to keep him whole.

He awaits my counsel. Carlyle demands an audience and I tremble at the thought of once again confronting the instrument of my torment. Yet my powers tell me that he fears me. I know this meeting shall be our last until I witness the moment of his death.

A part of me seeks vengeance now, longing to wield cold steel with the strength of my sorrow. I settle my thoughts on Carlyle and whisper a challenge to the wind which blows between our camps.

I know not when or how, yet I have foreseen he shall be vanquished for eternity. It is our destiny to oppose him and I know it is mine in this lifetime to defeat his purpose and keep my promises to Will.

Stephen, his chubby fingers fisted in anger, looks to me with his father's eyes. "I will help you, Mother. I can fight for you."

I fall to my knees, gathering my tiny daughter Serena and Stephen to my breasts. "As always, we shall protect one another. Our love will make us strong. Always."

As it is true that you and I who are one shall meet and fight for what is written in our stars.

Through the veil of time I have seen you who comes after me, and I have seen Carlyle beside you. He shall menace you with his evil. You must defy him and overcome his power. Believe this, for it will be true.

PART II:
Crescent Key, Florida–
Present Day

Chapter Nine

Deep beneath the water's surface, a diver gives up fighting the current and allows it to pull him where it will, faster and faster toward the depths of the ocean's floor. Then the invisible force frees him, and he hangs suspended over what looks like a dark shadow.

Could this be it?

His pulse speeds up. A shark circles below, and where there is one shark, there are many. But the lure is too strong to resist. Energized by instinct, he ignores the predator, kicks his flippers hard, and torpedoes closer.

As he spirals downward, the darkness starts to take shape, and he recognizes the culmination of his dreams—the hulk of the wreck he's been seeking.

Elated, he heads straight for it, and once there, skims along the rotting bones of what had once been a powerful British galleon. What is left of the warship lies scattered along the seafloor like a child's building blocks.

He looks about. The area is clear. The shark seems to have gone on to better hunting grounds. He skims a lone canon half-buried in the sand, then rounds what is left of the hull. Centuries of storms and tides have spread the remains, so he widens his search, circling the disjointed skeleton.

Suddenly his headlamp picks up a flicker of color yards from the main wreckage. Part of the mother lode? Could it be? His stomach knots, and he can hardly breathe. Drawn like a moth to a flame, he plunges toward the potential treasure.

Even as he reaches for what looks like a gold crescent encrusted with emeralds, another diver shoots out of nowhere, hand driving into the still-buried mother lode and coming up out of the sand with a bejeweled gold dagger.

He strikes out…

…the intended target the first diver's air hose.

Cordelia Ward awakened in a cold sweat, her wrist throbbing with heat, the yacht rocking gently beneath her.

Even as she twisted the Posey ring—now too tight— around her forefinger, praying to affect the outcome of the nightmare, she knew better. Precognitive dreams signaled by her birthmark had begun haunting her since her sixteenth summer, when a nightmare foretold the coming hurricane that scattered not only the mother lode of a shipwreck, but the lifelong aspirations of her museum-curator parents.

Her birthmark always burned, her ring always tightened, each time a dream opened the future to her.

Not so for an ordinary dream.

Fully awake now, too disturbed by the dream-vision to go back to sleep, she rose from her bunk, padded to one of the portholes and looked out over the water. The *Evening Star* was anchored in a cove for the night, their salvage boat a quarter mile down the coast. She looked out to sea, far out in the direction they would take in the morning. Lines of foam, generated by gentle waves, were encrusted in silver-blue moonlight.

The *Celestine* was out there somewhere under the transparent surface. Waiting. For her.

So, who were the divers she'd seen in the dream? Treasure hunters?

They were always something to fear for a marine archeologist about to make an important find. And she knew that find was imminent. Pirates could take everything right from under her nose if she didn't publicly claim the find first. Born to wealth, Cordelia didn't care about the money. The find itself, and what it meant to her family, was important to her.

She was really and truly awake, the night before perhaps the most important dive of her life. She glanced at the treasure box holding Elizabeth's journal but didn't have the emotional stamina to tackle new entries right now. Instead, she sat at her desk, turned on her laptop and sought the local news that had been televised earlier. If nothing else, she could get a confirmation that tomorrow's weather would hold.

She barely listened to stories about national politics or the state financial crisis or a local car accident. But her attention was riveted to the screen and a graphic that was a sketch of a centuries-old three-masted ship with the words *Sunken Treasures* crawled below it across the screen. The graphic cut to an attractive, dark-haired reporter standing at the water's edge.

"A native of this part of the state, Morgan Murphy has been plying these waters nearly his whole life. Tomorrow, he starts a new

hunt for sunken treasure."

Gasping, Cordelia turned up the volume as the camera pulled out to include the subject of the piece—a thirty-something-year-old male, long hair whipping around rugged features, open cotton shirt revealing ripped musculature.

"Morgan, what makes you think there's treasure in these waters?"

"I know there's treasure, Reya. I can smell it."

He displayed a set of perfect white teeth, his grin seemingly aimed straight at Cordelia. She clenched her jaw in response.

The reporter laughed. "Is that how you make your finds?"

"I have my methods."

"Which include?"

"Months of research before setting out, of course."

"So what exactly are you hoping to find this time, Morgan?"

"A ship that sank in these waters in 1605. The Celestine."

Cordelia's head went light and her pulse thundered. How was this possible? That now of all times, the man some called a pirate was after the same find as she? And *months* of research? Her father had spent years tracking the *Celestine*!

Her mind was whirling so that she barely heard the rest of the piece, and when the reporter said, *"Reya Delgado reporting from Crescent Key,"* Cordelia slammed the laptop's lid closed.

A noise above the cabin—the soft padding of bare feet on deck—told her that she wasn't the only one awake. Recognizing the light steps, she threw on a long-sleeved cotton shirt over the shorts and tank top that were her sleepwear, crossed through the galley, and took the steps that led her outside.

Her mother, Madelyn, stood at the rail, her moon-silvered blond hair fluttering around her face and shoulders. Thinking to tell her mother about the interview with the treasure hunter that had set her off-kilter, she hesitated.

"Something wrong, Mom?"

"Same as always. I long for your father."

"Me, too."

Knowing this was the wrong time—her mother would learn of their competitor soon enough—Cordelia leaned on the rail next to her mother and said nothing. Who knew where Murphy would start his hunt, anyway? He'd probably gotten wind of some bit of information and was charging after it. That didn't mean he would find the real site. *Her* site.

"Clive should be here for this," her mother said wistfully. "After losing *De Oro Del Casco*, he spent his life researching the *Celestine*."

De Oro Del Casco being the remains of the sunken Spanish galleon lost in the hurricane as her precognitive dream had foretold. Though she knew she hadn't made it happen, Cordelia couldn't help but feel some residual guilt.

She slipped her arm around her mother's waist. "It's because Dad did all that research that I was able to put together his notes and maps and find the *Celestine* for him. And for you."

At least she hoped she would beat Murphy to it.

Her mother hugged her tightly, and Cordelia pressed her cheek to her mother's forehead. Finding love the way her parents had seemed an abstract concept to her. She'd thought that maybe she was in love before but never long enough to be tested. Something inexplicable had always pulled her apart from the object of her affection.

Unfortunately, always obsessed with finding treasure

that would validate him as a museum curator, Clive Ward had also taken off on other, less researched, hunts. He'd gone on his last hunt the previous summer. Despite a brewing storm, Dad had chanced the dive never to resurface. Days of searching for his body had been for nothing.

Cordelia liked to think that her father was simply swimming with the sharks forever.

Thankfully, she still had her mother here with her. She clung to the knowledge that they were so close. Not all mothers and daughters shared what they had. Cordelia pulled away and smiled. Though Mom's heart-shaped face had softened and light lines crinkled around her blue eyes when she smiled in return, she was still the most beautiful woman Cordelia knew. People said they looked alike. Cordelia thought people were simply being kind.

Mom's smile faded, and she turned back to the sea. Her mother had been devastated by the loss of her husband. She'd given up her position at the museum. Had given up her social activities. Had given up her life. She'd become a recluse.

Without a center, Madelyn Ward had lost the will to go on.

Determined to restore that to her mother, Cordelia had lured her from grief-filled days to go hunting one last time, with the promise of completing her father's legacy. And, for the memory of her beloved Clive, Mom had agreed.

"I think we should both get some sleep," Cordelia said.

Mom nodded. "We go to the site tomorrow."

"And maybe find some artifacts."

They hugged again and went down to their separate cabins, but Cordelia didn't immediately go to her bunk.

The image of Morgan Murphy crowded her brain waves. Needing to distract herself from thinking about a potentially dreadful twist to the hunt, she opened the treasure box, slipped Elizabeth's journal from where it had hidden for four hundred years. She was halfway through Elizabeth's story. The more she read, the closer she felt to the most fearless woman she wished she somehow could have known.

Dunham Castle, 1601

My torment has deepened until it has become a part of me, making dark all my days. I see the same anguish in the duke's eyes, so like Will's and in my gentle Laurel's stricken face. I fear for her weakening body and soul. Even to her I cannot tell my secret. That I carry her beloved Will's child within my womb. None must know the truth until the time is right.

Now the time has come for me to face Carlyle with my rage and my power. He shall know my wrath and more which shall follow him through eternity.

Her eyes filling with tears at the double tragedy—Elizabeth losing the man she loved and then having to marry his murderer—Cordelia read until her eyes grew heavy and she could read no more. The birthmark on her wrist still throbbed slightly as she carefully placed the journal on a shelf next to her bunk and turned off the light. Every time she felt the weight of the journal in her hands, she felt Elizabeth come alive, almost as if her birthmark claimed them as being one somehow.

Staring at the moon that hung outside her porthole, she turned the Posey ring that had once belonged to each of the women in her family through the past four centuries, and thought of her inheritance.

A ring...

...a legend of love that spanned the ages...

...and a sometimes scary legacy connected to the birthmark on her wrist...

Tomorrow, they would sail to the location where she had pinned the wreck site. She would take the first dive.

She would beat the pirate to the site and stake her claim.

This could be a win-win situation if she found the mother lode. Her father's reputation would be restored, reviving her mother's will to live a full life—someone had to curate the find, after all, and why not Dr. Madelyn Ward?—and Cordelia's own future as a marine archeologist would be secured.

She wanted to someday be admired by a hoped-for daughter, to possess the same fearlessness of her ancestress Elizabeth.

What would she add to the box?

Hopefully something from the *Celestine*.

Hopefully this time her psychic instinct had been wrong...

Light and darkness often went hand in hand, as she well knew.

Darkness in the human form of a modern-day pirate had just complicated the hunt. The light was the treasure, but would she beat him to it? And then there was the jewel-encrusted dagger—both a prize from the *Celestine* and a weapon of evil.

Would another diver really be murdered for this mother lode?

Her birthmark said yes. She rubbed it as if she could soothe it away, as if she could change its mind, but it wouldn't yield. It burned hotter with her disturbed thoughts. Her ring grew so tight, she finally unseated it and then stared at the tiny treasure circling the tip of her finger.

Would Morgan Murphy do anything to secure the prize, no matter how depraved?

Not if she could help it.

Cordelia didn't want her success to come at the cost of a life.

But how could she prevent the tragedy she'd seen in her dream world?

Chapter Ten

The dream and the video interview haunted Cordelia the next morning as she prepared for the dive. Mom was in such a cheerful, hopeful mood that she kept all her worries to herself.

Immediately after breakfast, they put up sail and moved out, the salvage vessel, *Foley's Treasure*, following. She'd met Innis Foley during her hurricane summer. He'd been her first crush. It was somehow prophetic that they would unearth this find together. She'd hired him and his company on the spot when he'd sought her out after hearing rumors of her proposed expedition. With her father's maps to find the approximate location, they would use the ship's magnetometer to pinpoint the area with metal readings from the wreck's canons.

"How are your nerves?" he asked, his golden-brown gaze searching her face as they donned their vests and tanks.

Taking a look around, she didn't see another dive boat

on the horizon. Murphy would go to the wrong site. She had nothing to worry about.

Even so, she admitted, "My stomach is whirling a little more than normal. What if I've made a mistake? Or what if someone has actually beaten us to the find? Or what if the manifest was wrong and there is no real treasure aboard the *Celestine?*"

Which would devastate her mother if there was nothing to curate. If Cordelia was so inclined, she could always join another search.

Laughing, Innis slid a hand along her face and gazed deep into her eyes. A wave of copper-brown hair spilled over his forehead. "This is it, love. Believe in what you know. Don't ever doubt yourself."

A thrill shooting through her, Cordelia grinned at Innis. He'd given her exactly what she'd needed to regain her confidence.

"And if you are in want of extra luck," came a woman's accented voice as the Haitian cook joined them, "then take this with you."

Cordelia glanced at the feathered object in Brigitte's hand. The too-thin cook, whose long hair was braided and beaded in tiny rows, and her giant of a husband, Leandre, Innis's first mate, were island superstitious.

"I appreciate your making that for me, Brigitte, but taking it on the dive would no doubt ruin the pretty feathers."

The woman's dark features pulled as tight as her voice. "Up to you, cher."

"Take it," Innis urged as he secured the vest's straps over a chest that rippled with well-defined muscle.

"Of course." Though she didn't believe in the magic

of Voodoo fetishes, she didn't want to offend the woman. Besides, knowing they had competition for the treasure, she figured she could use all the luck she could get. Taking the little feathered object, she smiled. "Thank you for your good wishes."

Brigitte's lips curved. "You are welcome."

Cordelia slipped the fetish in her mesh ditty bag that was attached to her weight belt and took a moment as she always did before a dive to pray that she and her partner would remain safe throughout. Though the salvage vessel had a full crew including several divers, she was scheduled to take the first dive only with Innis.

With her dream beginning to replicate before her eyes, Cordelia could hardly breathe despite the full tank strapped to her back. She hung over the bones of the wreck, gaze darting around as if she would pin some knife-wielding villain in the shadows. All she saw were several nurse sharks, usually harmless, but enough to make the skin along her spine crawl even after the predators disappeared into the deep. A yank on her arm startled her, and she gazed into Innis's mask. He tilted his head toward the hull, and she followed. Taking a closer look at the area beneath her, she realized things looked quite different than they had in the dream world. The area hadn't been touched by human endeavor, at least not for nearly a century. Of course, her dream had shown her a site that had been worked on, which would happen when they used the magazine attached to the salvage ship to blow away sand.

In the meantime, she and Innis were merely making a discovery dive. Innis used an underwater camera to snap digital photographs that they could share with the crew before other divers came down that afternoon and started setting up a grid.

That might change the direction of her dream. There had been no grid in her vision. Perhaps, once her crew had set it up, that would negate the danger. Deep in her heart, she knew she was simply being hopeful. Her precognitive dreams weren't that specific to detail. The intent was what mattered.

Shoving away dark thoughts, she lost herself in the joy of the find, going down to the seafloor every so often to brush away sand from some object. Uncovering a canon with eroded lettering on its base, she could barely make out the name. *Celestine*. She *had* found it! Her pulse sped up, and she frantically searched for another canon. This was it, then, the culmination of her father's research. The high point of her own career. She became so focused that, as she backed up, she was startled again when Innis grabbed her, signaled her to stop, and pointed to something directly behind her. Realizing the birthmark on her wrist was burning, and her Posey ring tightening to warn her of danger, she carefully turned to look, and her heart began to thunder.

A ten-foot-long shark swam directly behind her. The thick body with tiger-like markings and a blunt snout told her it was a tiger shark. She felt paralyzed, unable to move.

Innis carefully inched her away from the potential danger.

He took her hand and squeezed hard, indicated they should surface—their air was running low anyway—and after the close call, she was having some difficulty breathing normally.

Innis had possibly saved her life.

She and Innis shared so many memories of the summer she'd been sixteen. Of her diving with her parents, while he salvaged with his father. Of a summer romance cut short when the impending hurricane forced her family to sail back to the Carolinas.

All those years since seemed to melt away.

When they broke the water's surface, Innis wrapped his arms around her and without warning, kissed her full on the mouth. A stunned, grateful Cordelia kissed him back but, still worried about the shark, quickly broke away.

Innis grinned at her, and her pulse fluttered as Leandre pull her up to the deck. The first mate winked at her, and behind him, Brigitte wore a satisfied expression, as if Innis had been part of the luck the cook had wished on her.

Her cheeks flooded with warmth, but, breathless, Cordelia couldn't help her happy smile. Innis was handsome, charming, and he'd just saved her from a possible shark attack. Plus there was the high of finding the wreck on the first dive. Who wouldn't smile?

"Are you all right?" Innis asked.

"Yes, I'm fine, thanks to you. If you hadn't been there…"

"Of course I was there. I'll always be there for you."

Now Cordelia grew uncomfortable as she always did when a man sounded like he meant to get serious about her. It wasn't that she didn't want someone in her life, but that she wanted the kind of relationship her parents had cherished. A soul mate. The problem was recognizing him.

Was he standing before her now?

The way Innis was devouring her with his eyes made her pulse thread unevenly. She took a big breath and ducked her gaze to her weight belt and the fetish, bright against the dark mesh of the ditty bag.

Relieving herself of her gear, she handed it over to one

of the crew. After which, she went straight to her mother, who stood near the door leading to the captain's quarters. Her expression carefully neutral, Mom twisted her hands together as if keeping herself from hoping too hard.

"This is it, Mom." Cordelia grinned. "We found one of the canons. It fit the description Dad had in his notes."

Her mother's lips parted and spread wide, as did her arms. Cordelia walked straight into them for a celebratory hug.

"So, what's this with Innis kissing you?" Mom whispered in her ear.

Cordelia kept her voice low. "He was just congratulating me."

She didn't want to worry her mother by telling her about the shark. Let Mom think it was part of the excitement of a successful dive.

When she turned around, Innis was heading straight for them, his pale brown eyes lit with something that reminded her of victory. Because he was certain they'd found the *Celestine*, or because he got to kiss her again?

Her pulse raced as she wondered what it would be like to let him do more than kiss her, to pick up where they'd left off years ago, when they were still young and innocent.

Innis stopped before them, sweeping his hair from his forehead with an open hand. His smile crooked, he then brushed a wet strand of hair from her cheek before looking at her mother.

"You should have been with us, Madelyn."

"Very kind of you, but I no longer dive."

Cordelia slipped her hand in her mother's and laced their fingers together. Mom hadn't gone in the water since her father's tragic last dive.

"A shame," Innis said. "But you'll get to see the site anyway. I took plenty of digital photos, and I'll be adding video footage to chronicle the entire underwater excavation. You'll get to see every detail."

"That would be wonderful!" Mom said, squeezing Cordelia's hand. "We can incorporate it into the exhibition later…" She hesitated a second. "…if this turns out to be the find that Clive thought it was, of course."

Innis grinned. "Ah, my dear Madelyn, I would venture we have reason to celebrate."

"I wouldn't be doing that all too soon," boomed a deep, familiar voice from behind him.

Cordelia looked over Innis's shoulder and gasped when she saw the man standing on the rail. Beard-stubbled, a large emerald in his right earlobe, his dark, shoulder-length hair windswept as if he were about to fly, he stood spread-legged, arms crossed over his broad tan chest. For a moment, she forgot to breathe. He was wearing nothing but a pair of tight, knee-length black pants that showed off his assets. Her heart thundered. He looked every bit the modern-day pirate he'd appeared to be in magazine articles and in television interviews like the one she'd seen the night before.

Morgan Murphy had found their site after all.

"What are you doing here, Murphy?" Innis demanded. "Lost your way again?"

"Actually, I've found it, Foley. I'm here to warn you to stay away from my family treasure."

Cordelia nearly choked on that. "*Your* family treasure?"

He jumped down from the rail, and in three long-legged strides stood staring down at her from eyes that gleamed, brilliant as the emerald earring. "You must be Cordelia Ward."

She backed up a step. He was so much bigger in person than on video, not only in size but in potency. Power seemed to roll off the pirate. She sucked in a breath. Not that he had any power over her, of course.

"And you must be that pirate, Morgan Murphy." Cordelia remembered the confidence he'd had in the telecast interview—he exuded even more in person. "Keep your distance from *my* family treasure!"

Wedged between the two men, she struggled to regain control of herself. Her heart was pounding and her birthmark seared her wrist, a sure warning of trouble. She stepped closer to Innis, certain that he and his armed crew would keep her safe.

Murphy arched an eyebrow at her. "If you want something out of this treasure hunt, you've chosen to align yourself with the wrong man."

"And what would make *you* the right man?" she demanded, denying the chemistry that confounded her.

"Nothing," Innis quickly said. "Get back to your own boat, Murphy, and head out of here, or I'll have my men throw you off!"

A quick look beyond the rail told Cordelia that Murphy had pulled his boat smack up against *Foley's Treasure*. Three tough-looking crewmen of the *Sea Rover* stood at the rail, seemingly ready for a fight. Innis's salvage crew appeared equally ready and willing to take them on.

"We're in international waters," Murphy reminded Innis. "And the treasure is under law of find. Finders keepers."

Cordelia was too familiar with the law of "finds." A finder obtained not only possession, but also ownership of the property when a discovered shipwreck was beyond the reach of the original owners. This applied to the *Celestine*. Or rather, it had.

"At least part of that mother lode is mine by law," Cordelia said. "It belonged to my ancestors, and I'm here to collect my family's inheritance."

Murphy cocked an eyebrow at her. "I suppose you can prove that."

"I have a copy of the original manifest—"

"As do I. That proves nothing."

"How did you get it, Murphy?" Innis's face flooded with angry color. "And the map, too. You must have gotten your hands on that or you wouldn't know where to look." He flashed an accusing look at his crew. Then to Murphy. "How did you steal the map from us?"

"Steal?" Murphy drew himself up and took a step closer so they were face-to-face, nose to nose. Innis stood six feet, but Murphy was even taller. "A fine accusation from a man who makes his living finding things that belong to other people and then holding them hostage until he's paid to give them back."

"I go by the book. You know very well salvage is a legitimate business."

"Pirating isn't," Cordelia added. "You aren't wanted here, Morgan Murphy."

As if suddenly remembering her, Murphy grinned and winked as if he didn't believe she was serious. Cordelia's mouth went dry, and she had as much difficulty breathing as when she'd caught sight of the shark. Her wrist was practically on fire now, and her Posey ring seemed to tighten…tighten….tighten around her finger.

"I'll get off this boat, Cordy—"

"Cordelia."

"Cordy," Murphy insisted. "And, I'll find the mother lode before you do."

Innis pushed between them and right into the other man's face again. "Not bloody likely."

"Don't underestimate me."

"Nor me!"

Cordelia gave her mother a frantic look but got no help there. Mom seemed hopelessly mesmerized by the argument.

"All right, enough!" Cordelia shouted.

Both men snapped to, giving her their full attention.

"Did anyone ever tell you how amazing you are when you're assertive?" Murphy asked. "More."

He was trying to get under her skin. And succeeding. Rubbing her burning wrist against her thigh, Cordelia forced herself to keep a neutral expression. "Arguing is a waste of energy. Who gets what will be decided underwater."

"Playing this out below the surface sounds good to me," Murphy said.

Innis stepped forward. "Cordelia, let me handle this—"

She put a hand on his chest to stop him, her focus on Murphy. "Whatever we find will have historical significance. Such treasures belong in a museum where they can be appreciated by everyone."

"And when I find the mother lode and collect the treasure, maybe I'll even create my *own* museum to show it off to the public."

Of course. He wasn't only after the money but the glory that would accompany such an incredible find. Irritated by the media-loving, rogue treasure hunter—a slightly nicer title than pirate—Cordelia refused to let him bait her again.

Seeming disappointed, Murphy bowed his head, first to her, then to her mother, then bounded to the rail and jumped from one boat to another. He nearly did fly and landed lightly on the other rail. One look back—a wink at Cordelia—and he jumped down to the deck.

Cordelia stared after him, her mouth agape.

"Well, wasn't that something," Mom said, sounding a little dazed.

"Don't worry, Madelyn, we won't let that pirate or his crew steal Ward thunder." Innis wrapped a possessive arm around Cordelia's shoulders. "We have more divers than he does. We won't ever leave him or his men alone in the water to steal what isn't his."

Ward thunder.

Her father's dream.

That was right. Cordelia wasn't going to let anyone steal that from him. Or from her mother. Or from herself.

She watched the *Sea Rover* move a hundred yards away from *Foley's Treasure* and drop anchor, then realized she was focused on the boat's captain. Something about Morgan Murphy got to her. No doubt it had simply been the excitement of the hunt followed by the shock of his sudden appearance.

She leaned into Innis and he tightened his hold on her somewhat possessively.

The heated exchange between him and Murphy and her had been quite stimulating while happening. But now that things had quieted down, the dream vision invaded her thoughts once more, and her wrist burned even hotter.

Murphy might be a pirate...but a killer?

Dread that she couldn't shake filled her, until it came to

Cordelia. She knew what she had to do.

First find the treasure.

Then find the dagger itself so that she could destroy it before its malevolent promise could be fulfilled.

Chapter Eleven

Determined that he would get the best of the salvager and his wealthy employer, a furious Morgan moved his smaller, less reputable-looking craft just far enough from *Foley's Treasure* and the *Evening Star* to have some privacy. Just thinking about Cordelia Ward set him off, and not just because she defied him and presented an obstacle to his hunt. There was something about the woman that set his juices flowing, that made him want her to want him…

"So what do you think, boss?" his first mate, Emmett Green, asked.

"That we're in for a fight."

Though he would get the best of Cordelia Ward yet.

Spoiled little rich girl.

Like her parents before her, she had the money necessary to do whatever it took to get what she wanted. The "haves" always thought it was their right to have more. Not this time, not while he was still breathing. For some reason, the thought of challenging Cordelia—Cordy—made his blood rush at dizzying speeds. He felt as if he knew her, had always desired her, which was, of course, ridiculous.

Determined not to let her influence his goal, he said, "We have to be smarter and faster and more aggressive than that pair."

"Big order, considering how few men we got compared to them," Emmett noted.

True, being that there was Cordelia and Foley and a half-dozen men. He was two men down. One of his divers had just up and disappeared after their last hunt. Considering they'd come away with nothing, Morgan couldn't blame him.

And then there was Emmett.

The first mate couldn't dive any more. A three-pack-a-day man, Emmett had smoked until a doctor had strapped an oxygen tank to his back—not so that he could dive, but simply to help him breathe since he'd developed emphysema. Emmett wasn't breathing in oxygen now, but there were times the old man had no choice. Morgan couldn't fire him. Who else would give a man his age, in his condition, a job? Besides, Emmett was still useful—he took care of the equipment, managed the dives from topside, and fed Morgan and the other men three squares a day. He earned his keep.

"At least for the time being, until we find the mother lode, we'll have to make do with four divers," Morgan said, including himself in the count.

"Half the number on the Ward woman's dive team."

"There's no helping it."

"You could try for an investor—"

Morgan glared at Emmett, stopping his first mate mid-sentence. Then he entered the main cabin of the *Sea Rover*.

He would never beg anyone for money. He'd seen his father do it over and over, most of his life, changing him from a proud man to one always oozing gratitude, usually to some stranger. One of the myriad "haves" in this world like Cordelia Ward. Morgan would be his own man, make his own name, and then others could come to him for money. He would never make someone who had a dream beg for his help.

As he looked over his maps and notes spread over his desk, he kept glancing out the porthole, watching the other crew's activities as they got ready to dive. He speculated on the best moves to thwart the Ward woman. He and his men could simply dive where they were anchored and take advantage of the area cleared by Foley's magazine. Of course that could start an all-out war. Someone could get hurt, and there were sure to be repercussions. He didn't need that. No, he had to play it smart, keep his men just far enough away from hers to keep an uneasy peace.

At least until he had reason to do otherwise.

How in the world had Cordelia Ward found the *Celestine's* wreck her first time out, when he'd been seeking it for years and only recently narrowed the search area after getting his hands on a century-old map he'd found in a musty island antique shop?

While his parents Daniel and Jane had always maintained they were content with their lot, despite living in too small quarters, taking temporary jobs, and begging for money from backers, Morgan wanted more for himself and for them. Not just money but recognition. They'd given their lives to the search, would have kept at it if they'd ever been rewarded, if they hadn't been cheated by a greedy backer. He had a much tougher attitude. His siblings had gotten out of the life, as well, but truth be told, Morgan lived for the hunt—well, most of what was involved, anyway.

And now that he was so close to getting everything he'd ever wanted—everything his parents had been denied for more than three decades—he wasn't about to let a rich newcomer snatch the prize from under his nose. Once he had his hands on the mother lode, he would be the treasure-hunting star of the media, and wealthy backers who'd made his father beg would seek him out, glad to fund him for other ventures.

He pulled the ring from a drawer and examined it once more. Every time he touched it, it filled him with the surety that he would succeed this time. It also made him feel things he didn't want to acknowledge.

Emotions…and dreams that felt almost real.

Nothing specific. Just a glimpse here and there of places and people foreign to him. A woman with dark hair, tending to one more fragile than she. What looked like a medieval castle. Men on horses. The dark-haired woman again, this time tending to a small boy.

He got glimpses of her when awake, as well, like memories long buried.

Handling the ring as if he could pry open its secrets, he could almost see the woman now, almost hear the lilt of her soft voice whispering in the dark…

Could almost feel her loving touch on his cheek…

As if the ring had a life of its own…

"Aahh!" The frustration got to him and he curled his fingers around the ring.

Next he fetched his newest treasure, a gold chain set with diamonds, from which hung a sapphire-studded crescent moon. He'd found it by luck when he'd gone down alone and had sifted through the sand by hand. The chain obviously had been torn from a larger piece, one he hadn't yet found.

A matter of time and opportunity.

Certain the find would be his, he tucked both ring and chain away again.

Glaring out the porthole at his competition, Morgan decided he would do whatever it took, even if he had to get close to Cordelia Ward for information. The idea of getting really close to her made his blood rush even faster—she was a beautiful, exciting woman. He wanted a taste of that. But would a taste be enough for him? Not that his desires would let her stop him from getting what he deserved.

If her claim had any validity, Morgan wasn't aware of it. His research had proved this particular sunken treasure was *his* family's inheritance, therefore fate decreed that he should be the one to claim it.

Everything Innis Foley ever wanted was within his reach.

If Morgan Murphy didn't foul things up for him, that was.

"I told you the fetish would do its work on the woman," Brigitte said in a low voice from behind him, though they were alone in the galley.

"So you did." He turned to meet her dark gaze. "You kept your promise."

"As I assume you will keep yours."

"You know I always pay for what I want."

"Good," she murmured. "Then we will have no problem."

"What kind of problem would that be?"

Did she think to use her Voodoo on him? Innis knew he shouldn't put it past her.

As if reading his mind, Brigitte tilted her head and gave him her most innocent expression. "I foresee only success where you are concerned."

"Good."

"Especially where your Cordelia is concerned, eh?"

"I've wanted her forever," he admitted. "I fell in love with her more than a decade ago when we were teenagers. And then, at summer's end, her parents took her home after a hurricane struck and destroyed the site of the wreck her father was diving. I thought I had lost her forever."

Two years older than Cordelia, he had gone off to college. Fate had kept them apart for many years, but he'd never gotten her out of his heart.

"Now you will finally have your heart's desire," Brigitte said. "Along with the treasure of a lifetime."

"Finding the mother lode and bringing it up for her will make her happy." When they'd met again a few years ago, she had treated him only like a good friend. He was desperate to change that. "I'm going to prove that I'm the right man for her."

They walked out on deck together.

Already suited up, his first mate stopped what he was doing and smiled when he saw his wife. "Brigitte, you are here for a good luck kiss before I go down, I assume?"

"Exactly."

Brigitte swayed over to the man who was more than double her width and stood on her toes for that kiss. And Innis couldn't help envying Leandre, though he told himself that it was only a matter of time before he had such power over Cordelia's feelings.

Two teams ready to go down were doing a final check on their equipment

"Get that magazine going," he told Leandre, who took charge of the blowers, the main tool they would use to clear the area so the divers could see what they had below.

Leandre lowered the giant tubes mounted on the stern. As they plunged downward into the blue-green depths, Innis told the divers, "Get in that water and find the first of the treasure before that pirate does."

"And be careful!" Cordelia yelled over the noise of the magazine engine.

She looked stunning standing there at the rail of the *Evening Star* next to her mother. Still wearing her turquoise bathing suit, she'd wrapped a flower-print sarong around her and tied it at her hips. Her feet were bare, her blond hair was free, an errant breeze fluttering the pale strands around her lightly tanned face. He'd never seen anything more beautiful. Just looking at her when she was unaware of his scrutiny made it hard to breathe.

Cordelia Ward was everything he'd ever wanted in a wife. And Innis was certain she was destined to be his.

He joined them at the rail. "I have a good feeling about this." Cordelia turned to look up him. Her eyes shone with expectation. "I do, too."

"We make a good team."

"Of course. Exactly as good friends should."

"I need to see to lunch," Madelyn said, leaving the rail. "Would you care to join us, Innis?"

"I would love to." He waited until she was out of earshot before saying, "I've dreamed of this day, Cordelia."

She nodded. "Finding the *Celestine* was Dad's dream, so I understand."

"I meant working side by side with you."

She flushed. "You've dreamed of it?"

"Ever since we were so tragically separated all those years ago."

"Why, I do believe you're being a bit dramatic, Innis Foley," she said in a teasing voice that made him smile.

"Only a little."

He knew he had it in him to do whatever he set his mind to. He'd already proved that he was the right man to run Foley Salvage, the family business. His father had made him feel unworthy—had tried to convince him that he would turn out to be nothing—but, determined to get ahead, Innis had hardened himself against his own uncertainty. In the end, he'd won over the board and had defeated his acrimonious father. Taking control of the business, he'd proved the old man wrong.

A first step in the right direction for his future.

This treasure hunt was his chance to get everything he ever wanted, starting with Cordelia and ending with the infamous celestial girdle, the jeweled prize of the *Celestine* mother lode.

After all, who had a better right to claim it than a descendant of the House of Lennox?

• • • • •

Cordelia was furious when Morgan shadowed her team and sent his divers down so close to hers as they investigated the hulk. She'd felt like they were looking over her shoulder for an opportunity to claim what she might find.

She couldn't wait to go down again for a second dive, but Innis was busy supervising via a live video feed from one of his divers equipped with an underwater camera. She didn't want to dive with anyone else, at least not today. After watching the monitor over Innis's shoulder, she caught sight of more sharks. Twice in one day was enough for her, and they did have six divers.

She wandered across deck to where her mother sat in a shady spot.

Mom glanced up at her. "You seem tense."

"Nervous. I should be down there with the other divers."

"Then why aren't you?"

Cordelia looked to the navigation area where Innis had set up the monitors. "My dive partner is otherwise occupied."

"So that's it, is it?"

"What do you mean?"

"You're interested in Innis."

"Of course I am."

"I remember the summer when you two met and hung out together. He seemed to make you happy."

"He did." Cordelia felt the attraction she'd had all those years ago spring back to life, but the project came first. As always.

"Then you'll be giving a personal relationship another chance?"

She took the seat next to her mother. "We'll see."

"No man has ever had the power to come before your work."

"Perhaps because the right man wasn't around to distract me properly."

"Cordelia, if you don't have feelings for Innis—"

"But I *do* have feelings for him," Cordelia argued. "I just need to sort them out."

She'd never forgotten the boy who'd first kissed her, who'd held her heart for a summer, but when she had a specific goal, she was single-minded until she reached it. Finding the *Celestine's* mother lode was her current focus. Not that she didn't want romance in her life. Until now, it had simply been an abstract concept. Innis was making her wonder what working together would bring in terms of their personal relationship. He was so confident and had a dynamic personality. What woman wouldn't be flattered by his interest?

"If you do care for Innis, what do you intend to do about it?"

"It's too soon, Mom. I have to get to know him all over again. Innis and I haven't even spent any time alone together since he agreed to work the hunt for us."

"You'll have this evening at the Crescent Key Yacht Club. I'm not up to going to the festivities, after all."

Cordelia had been looking forward to Midsummer Night, to celebrating the Summer Solstice, her birthday, and a night of magic, echoing whispers of her supernatural inheritance from Elizabeth. But if her mother didn't want to go...

"Mom, you have to come."

"I know it's your special day, but I'd rather not leave the ship. Out here, I feel closer to Clive than I have since he died. It's a wonderful feeling."

"Then I won't go, either. I'll stay here with you and—"

"Give me some room, honey. I'm glad you got me here. Remembering all those hunts with your father is filling my heart. I need a little time alone with his memory. You understand, don't you?"

"Of course." Though she didn't. Not really. Not when she'd never experienced the kind of love and commitment her parents had had for each other.

"Then stop pushing, please. I want you to have a good time with Innis. The best birthday ever."

Though Cordelia knew she had, indeed, been pushing her mother to rise up from the depression that had taken over her life, she still wasn't certain if her mother was insisting on the time alone for herself or to let her daughter have time alone with a special man. Either way, she was going to respect her mother's request for her to stop pushing. But while on the subject of her father...

"How did you know Dad was the right man for you?"

A sad smile slipped across her mother's lips. "From the moment we met, I couldn't imagine my life without him."

Words that had recently seared her heart. "Elizabeth said the same about Will."

"You've been reading her journal again."

"Last night. She talks about a love that will live through the ages." She could almost hear Elizabeth's heartfelt message, as if she'd been there. "I can't imagine ever feeling such emotion. And yet I feel connected to her."

"She was our ancestor."

"Four centuries ago. It's difficult to explain, but I feel like she's here now, with me somehow."

"The journal has touched your heart." Mom picked up Cordelia's hand and kissed the birthmark on her wrist. "You are special, my lovely daughter. Never forget that. You have her mark."

While the Posey ring and treasure box had been passed down from mother to daughter for four centuries, the birthmark, along with psychic ability, skipped generations.

"Do you ever regret not having the connection?" Cordelia asked.

"I had your father to keep me content. The women who have borne the mark haven't always fared well in love."

"You think there's a connection?" One that affected her?

"Who is to say? You're an exceptional woman. Anything is possible for you. Perhaps you hold Elizabeth's magic as well."

Oh, sure. The biggest trick Cordelia had ever managed was a little telekinesis.

Not that moving things around with her mind was easy for her.

The last time was several months ago, when she'd sent a vase of flowers flying against a wall. Her supposed date had them delivered after standing her up when he'd told her to meet him in front of a movie theater.

Spotting a magazine that had fallen to the deck of her mother's chair, Cordelia concentrated on it, willed it to move back where it belonged. A couple of pages fluttered—her or the breeze?—and Cordelia gave up. She'd been trying to make telekinesis work for her off and on all her life, but it seemed that strong emotions had to be involved or she simply couldn't do it.

"Magic, huh?" she mused. "That would be great if it translated into my finding the mother lode before that treasure hunter gets his hands on it." On the knife with the jeweled handle in particular.

"I'm glad you found the journal, but don't get lost in the romance of Elizabeth's story."

Having told her mother about several of the journal entries, Cordelia wondered what bothered her. "Why the warning?"

"If Elizabeth's belief that she and Will shall find each other again is true, then Carlyle shall certainly try to stop them from being together."

Despite the icy fingers that crept down her spine, Cordelia laughed. "C'mon, Mom. Elizabeth was the ultimate romantic. That's not me. I'm far too pragmatic to believe in such a haunting love story."

She glanced at Innis, walking toward them with a sparkle in his eyes and a smile hovering about the lips that had kissed her.

And for a heart-tripping moment, she wondered if it could all be true.

Chapter Twelve

Later that afternoon, several crew members from *Foley's Treasure* were getting ready to go down for the last dive of the day. And Innis was going with them.

"Maybe I should join you." An anxious Cordelia didn't want to miss anything. She wasn't one to sit mesmerized watching a video feed for an entire dive. "I have only done that one dive this morning."

"Save your energy for tomorrow when the hunt really begins." Innis did a final check on his regulator and slipped into his vest and tank. "It's up to you, but I thought you might want to spend some time this afternoon with your mother, being that she'll stay onboard alone tonight."

Even though Mom had insisted, Cordelia couldn't help but feel a little guilty. "You do have a point."

"And I have enough divers to finish setting up the grid. I promise you, that's all we'll do today." Grinning at her, Innis leaned close enough that she could feel his breath on her cheek. "I wouldn't think of searching for treasure without you."

A little breathless, she said, "All right, then."

Still, she glanced over to her greatest worry—the *Sea Rover*, anchored but a hundred yards away.

"And don't give Murphy another thought, Cordelia." Innis's brow furrowed and his mouth tightened. "If he becomes a problem, I'll take care of him."

Did he mean physically? Cordelia hoped not.

"Innis, please don't do anything foolish. I wouldn't want you to get hurt."

"How do you know *I* would be the one hurt?"

"In-n-nis!"

"All right." He smiled at her. "I'll take it as a compliment that you're concerned about me. I won't do anything foolish."

He brushed his lips over hers in a kiss so quick she didn't have time to react. Then he saluted her and joined the members of his crew who were making the dive.

Cordelia crossed back to the *Evening Star*, which was still anchored against *Foley's Treasure*. But rather than joining her mother immediately, she watched the divers roll into the water, wishing she were going with them. She couldn't keep herself from standing at the rail for long enough that she wondered what was going on below the surface.

Again, she checked out the *Sea Rover*. The only person visible was an older man who watched the waters with what seemed to be a sharp eye.

"Aaah!" Cordelia vented her frustration.

Certain that Murphy and his men were still down below and trying to beat her to the treasure, she only hoped they didn't find anything. And that they didn't make trouble for

Innis or his crew. Why couldn't this have been the idyllic treasure hunt she'd hoped for? Her father's memory deserved to be honored. Her mother deserved to have a reason to truly regain her life.

Surely Murphy wouldn't succeed in stealing that from the people she loved.

As if thinking about the treasure hunter had summoned him, Murphy rose up next to the boat like Poseidon emerging from the sea. Shocked by his presence, Cordelia stared down at him, openmouthed, stomach tightening, as he used the dive ladder to climb aboard. Not that he'd been diving. She thought he'd just swam over from his boat. He wasn't sporting any gear. Or much in the way of anything else. His short skins were tight enough to show off his trim waist and muscular thighs. And, well, all his assets.

Her mouth went dry.

He shook his head as if trying to clear his ears. Water whipped from his long hair and pelted her.

"Thanks for the shower, Murphy!" she forced out. "What do you think you're doing, boarding my boat without permission?"

And why was her pulse thundering so hard?

His lips quirked. "Would you have granted me permission?" When she didn't answer, he said, "That's what I thought. I wanted a chance to talk to you without Foley around to interrupt."

"Innis Foley is—"

"Your partner, right? Or is he something more?" His tone changed slightly. "Lover?"

How dare he ask her something so personal? That she'd hired Innis and had given him a stake in the find was her own business. "What we are—or aren't—is none of your concern."

Although his asking sent a trickle of awareness through her, made her wonder if he was interested in her personally. He was a fine-looking specimen, but she didn't want to be blinded to his real purposes by something as mundane as lust. She had to consider the man himself, just as she did Innis. She couldn't forget about Innis.

"So your relationship is strictly business," he went on.

"I didn't say that."

"You didn't say otherwise, either."

He punctuated the last with a smile. No, more of a smirk, really. Cordelia's knees grew soft and she covered by gripping the rail.

"What is your point, Murphy? Why did you want to speak with me?"

"I wanted to know if you would be reasonable."

"Reasonable? About the site? After all the years my father put into finding the *Celestine*?"

"But your father didn't find it."

"Because he died first. Tragically."

"On another dive." He nodded. "I read about it. My condolences."

Mollified just a little that he sounded sincere, she calmed herself down. "I'm taking up his cause, making his dream come true. A find like that would grace any museum."

"Or a museum could be built to house it."

"A museum with a stiff entry price?" she asked.

"Why not?"

"I'm not in this for the money."

"You can afford to have a disdain for money when you

haven't had to work your butt off to get enough for the hunt, wondering if it will even happen."

"I'm not going to apologize because I come from money."

"And I'm not going to apologize because I don't," he said, took a breath and then added, "Now, about my proposal. Will you agree to be reasonable?"

Flustered by the argument, she tensed. "What do you mean by reasonable?"

"I'm not going away."

"I got that, Murphy."

"I want to know if we can be friendly competitors."

"How friendly?" she asked, suddenly edgy.

"No dirty tricks. No sabotage. No violence."

Cordelia was appalled that he would think she would resort to anything so underhanded. "No one has ever accused me or my family of any of those things before!"

"I wasn't accusing you. However, Innis Foley could be a loose cannon. The reason I wanted to know your relationship status. Do you have a leash on him or not?"

A leash? Now Cordelia was getting angry. "Go away, Murphy. I'm not even going to respond to your insults. Get off my boat!"

"As you wish." He backed up to the rail and hopped on. "Just know that if you don't keep Foley and his men in line...well, I can give as good as I get!" With that, he rolled backward into the water.

For a moment, Cordelia watched him swim toward the *Sea Rover*. It was only then she realized her wrist hadn't burned, nor had her ring tightened the way they had when he'd shown up that morning. Did that mean he *wasn't* a danger? Or had he'd simply caught her off guard?

Determined not to let the treasure hunter have any power over her, she turned away and nearly ran into her mother.

"I heard the argument."

"I'm sorry if we disturbed you, Mom."

"You have no reason to be sorry."

"You're right. The man is a lout."

"Well, at least you didn't call him a pirate again. I don't think he is a pirate. Or a lout. I think he has history…not all good. I've heard more than a few tales of underhanded behavior among treasure hunters. Perhaps he has reason to fear being victimized somehow."

"Morgan Murphy is no victim."

"No, I can't imagine he ever has been. But he's been in the business for a very long time, since he was a child at his mother's knee. He comes from a family of treasure hunters. Lovely parents—Clive and I met the Murphys once—but they're nothing like their son. They might have his sense of purpose, but they don't have his strength. I believe he had to work at it consciously to be so certain of himself. Who knows what experience has played into his history?"

An observation that sobered Cordelia.

Had Murphy developed a persona that made him look like a pirate as a defense, as a means of self-protection?

Or was she fooling herself, creating a story to make him seem more acceptable?

Only time would tell.

The seductive evening and being with Innis, a man who obviously was infatuated with her, drugged Cordelia into being giddy, open to new possibilities. Despite seeing flashes in her mind's eye of Murphy in those tight diving skins, she focused on Innis, concentrated on the man with whom she had history.

The Crescent Key Yacht Club was the perfect setting for Midsummer Night, the perfect way to rekindle an old romance. Innis had reserved a table on the terrace where they could see the band that provided atmospheric music. In his tropical white suit and bronze shirt, he was positively mouth-watering. The perfect escort, he wined and dined and charmed her. She couldn't remember feeling so carefree since her father died.

"That music is tempting, don't you agree?" he asked of the slow Latin number the band was now playing.

"Mmm, indeed."

He held out his hand. "I can't resist the urge to hold you close with a breeze ruffling your hair and moonlight casting its glow over your lovely features."

Cordelia bit back a laugh and made do with a smile even if she thought Innis was being overly dramatic with his compliments.

"Such a romantic," she murmured.

"And I hope it's catching," he said, leading her to the terrace and pulling her into his arms.

Cordelia let herself soften in his arms, gave him the lead. They danced mere yards from the musicians. A sultry breeze shimmered around them, twirling the delicate hibiscus-print skirts of her backless dress so the material tangled around their legs. The sky was clear, the waning moon set in a swath of stars. Candlelight glowed from nearby stands and tables. Though it was cool near the water, she was heating up, thinking of how they would have the yacht to themselves on the way back to the site. Her mother had stayed behind on *Foley's Treasure*.

"Happy birthday," Innis murmured in her ear.

"Mom squealed on me!"

He grinned at her. "She did. I even bought a bottle of champagne to celebrate on the *Evening Star* later."

"What a perfect evening."

"What a perfect partner."

"Really? I'm a little rusty—"

"I didn't mean the dance." He returned his mouth to her ear. "I meant the woman."

Warmth flushed through her and she couldn't help but remember her conversation about romance with her mother. "You flatter me."

"I mean to. I've never gotten over you, Cordelia. That summer we spent diving together and lying around on the beach and talking about our dreams for our futures was unforgettable. I'll never forgive Hurricane Ella for destroying that wreck site and taking you away from me."

Cordelia remembered those days fondly. "I thought my heart was broken when we left for home. But really, we were so young."

"I was old enough to know what I wanted. From the moment I met you, I knew you were the woman for me. I haven't changed my mind."

Another echo from the journal.

Cordelia's chest tightened and her pulse picked up. Could it be? She felt closer than ever to Elizabeth. She suddenly knew that with all her heart she yearned for the kind of love that Elizabeth and Will had shared.

The way Innis was looking at her…the way his face edged closer to hers…Certain he was about to kiss her, she wet her lips, left them parted, half held her breath as she waited for his mouth to descend on hers.

And then her wrist began to burn.

She jerked slightly in his arms.

His expression immediately concerned, Innis asked, "What is it?"

Her ring tightened.

"I'm not sure…"

And then she was.

She couldn't miss Morgan Murphy, leaning against the terrace railing. Watching her. He looked every bit the pirate tonight. Tight black pants, black leather boots, full-sleeved white shirt billowing in the breeze, shoulder-length hair tied back with a strip of leather.

Innis stiffened. "What the hell is Murphy doing here?"

"I guess you'll have to ask him yourself," Cordelia said, as Murphy left the railing, his gaze locked onto hers.

Her wrist burned hotter, the Posey ring tightened… tightened…tightened…warning her of impending danger. Her heart began to thud and her throat felt like it had gone solid. She couldn't even swallow.

"Seems he wants to say something to us." Innis stopped dancing. "I'll take care of him."

Not that he had a chance.

The moment Innis drew himself together and let go of Cordelia, the treasure hunter swooped down on her and wrapped an arm around her waist.

"C'mon, Cordy, let's call a truce."

"It's Cordelia," she ground out through clenched teeth.

He swept her onto the dance floor away from Innis. She glanced back in time to catch the other man's murderous expression. For a moment, she thought Innis would come after them and start a scene. Then he seemed to get hold of himself and went straight to the bar.

Annoyed that her romantic evening had been interrupted, she demanded, "Now what do you want?"

"Can't I simply want to dance with a beautiful woman?"

"I would have to trust you to believe that."

"No trust? You wound me."

She lifted an eyebrow. "What is the real reason, Murphy?"

"Morgan to you," he said.

"Fine. Morgan."

"Maybe I just want to get to know my competition a little better—"

"Now *that* I believe."

"—to give you another chance to enter into a reasonable bargain with me."

Cordelia had an idea of how to protect her find. If it was money he wanted...

He held off the thought with a series of complicated turns and dips. Cordelia had to concentrate to keep up with him. They danced in perfect harmony, as if they'd been partners before. She felt the pulse in her throat as he led her closer and closer to the railing and the sea and farther and farther away from the crowd.

And then the music changed and he slowed to a near stop, barely more than rocking as he stared down into her face.

Flushing at the unexpected sensations shooting through her, Cordelia somehow found her voice. "What if I offer you a deal?"

A breeze blew her hair across her face. He smoothed away the errant strand and tucked it behind her ear. "What kind of deal?"

His fingers left a trail of sensation everywhere they touched her.

"A lucrative one," she choked out.

"Keep talking."

"How much would it take for you to lose interest in the *Celestine*?"

"Money?" His expression offended, he stopped moving. "There isn't enough."

"But now you have no guarantees that you'll sail away with anything. I can change that, make sure you have enough to start another hunt."

"You mean like an investor?" His voice dripped with sarcasm. "Does money normally buy you everything you want? You can't buy me, Cordelia Ward. No one can."

Cordelia gaped at him. He was actually acting insulted. Why, when he was in the hunt for the money? Or maybe that wasn't his motivation. Maybe it was the fame that went along with the fortune, the glory of being the one to find a four-hundred-year-old sunken treasure.

He leaned into her so close his breath laved her face. "How about I make you an honest offer—a partnership."

She stuck her right hand against his chest and backed off. "I don't think so. You and I have very different goals."

"I thought we both wanted to find the mother lode of the *Celestine*."

"I'm a marine archeologist and—"

He captured her hand before she could remove it. "And

I'm a pirate?"

"I didn't say that, but you are looking for treasure, while I am looking for artifacts."

"Not that I see the difference, but how about I offer you this." From his pocket, he pulled a diamond-studded gold chain from which hung a crescent moon set with sapphires.

Cordelia's eyes widened.

"Exactly." He took her right hand from where he'd trapped it and placed the artifact in her palm.

The touch of metal and jewels to her ring electrified Cordelia. Startled, she gasped at the power but wrapped her fingers around the jeweled moon so she wouldn't drop it. Her heart beating too fast, she took a closer look and recognized its age. This was no modern copy of something old.

Fearing that Morgan had found this on his earlier dive, would somehow beat her to the mother lode, she panicked. "All right, partners, then, but we need to work out details—"

Before she could finish, Morgan curled his fingers over her hand with the crescent and kissed her.

Her wrist burned.

Her ring tightened.

Her head went light.

The chain trapped between their hands connected them like a live wire, kept them from pulling apart. The current spread to every pore of her body, to her head, to her toes, to her feminine center.

She had never felt so alive, so sure of herself.

Until the kiss ended.

Looking up into Morgan's eyes that gleamed emerald with satisfaction, she had only one thought: What had she done? A treasure hunter was the last person who should attract her. They held opposing life values. She wanted to preserve the past, and he wanted to profit from it. He was so obviously focused on money, why wouldn't he take hers?

Confused and angry that he'd taken advantage of her emotions, she stepped away from him and looked around to see Innis approaching them.

"Just what do you think you're doing, Murphy?" he demanded.

"Sealing a deal." Morgan grinned at Innis. "Cordy just accepted my offer of a partnership."

"What?"

Morgan reached for her, but instinct made her whip his hand away using nothing more than her anger and her mind. His whole arm flew back hard, twisting his body, and her heart thundered in response.

Morgan's eyes went wide and questioning. "What the hell, Cordy?"

Cordelia realized he knew she'd been responsible. Just as when she'd sent that vase of flowers crashing against the wall, her telekinesis had turned on without her thinking due to her advanced emotional state.

Not wanting to give Morgan a chance to question her, she put a hand on Innis's arm. "Please take me back to the boat."

"I thought you wanted to work out the deal," Morgan said.

"Tomorrow." Realizing she still had the crescent and its chain in her hand, she held out the artifact to him

"No. You keep it as a token of good faith."

Innis's eyes widened as he got a good look. And then he glared at Morgan. "Where the hell did you get that?"

Morgan's lips quirked into a mysterious, irritating smile. "Tomorrow."

With that, he walked away and disappeared into the crowd, leaving her weak-kneed and confused.

"Are you all right, Cordelia? Murphy didn't do anything to force you to agree to this...this...partnership?"

"No, of course not." But the evening really was ended for her. "Please, let's get out of here."

Innis put his arm around her shoulders and led her off the terrace and toward the dock where the *Evening Star* was anchored. She tried to take comfort from his nearness, but her earlier romantic mood eluded her.

The electric kiss with the treasure hunter kept filling her thoughts instead.

"Can I ask why you agreed to a partnership with that pirate?" Innis asked.

Her hand tightened around the jeweled moon. "Because I feared he was too close to the mother lode, and if I didn't agree, he would get it all. No artifacts for a real collection."

No curator needed, depriving her mother of a reason to get up in the morning. No recognition for the father who had spent his life tracking down the very treasure that had belonged to her ancestors. No recognition for herself as a marine archeologist.

If she hadn't agreed, the glory would all go to the treasure hunter.

"You don't even know that he found that thing today. I didn't hear any celebration coming off his boat."

"If that's true..." Her mind raced with possibilities. Had Morgan somehow tricked her? "Then what have I done?" she asked aloud this time.

"Nothing wrong," Innis assured her, helping steady her as she took off her heels before getting onto the boat.

A moment later, they stood at the prow of the *Evening Star*. Innis took her in his arms, and she wished their evening had never been interrupted. Here was a man she could count on. A man she could trust. Maybe even a man she could love again.

"I will protect you and your interests, whatever it takes," Innis promised, his head angling toward hers. "I want nothing more than to make you happy."

This time his mouth met hers. Cordelia tried to lose herself in the kiss, but even as she kissed him in return, her mind was too aware that her wrist wasn't burning, that her ring wasn't tightening. By the time she realized that was a good thing, Innis ended the kiss, though he still held her in his arms.

"Whatever you need." His voice was gruff.

She needed to forget that electric kiss on the terrace.

Realizing Innis was waiting for some response, she said, "Thank you for that. Let's get back to the wreck site."

Remembering she'd had thoughts of their being alone on the boat with that bottle of champagne, she knew now that nothing was going to happen between them tonight.

Chapter Thirteen

The first thing Cordelia searched out when they dropped anchor was Morgan's boat. No lights. Subdued voices. No Morgan himself. Was he there below or still on Crescent Key plotting against her?

Innis kissed her again before going straight over to *Foley's Treasure*, leaving her confused and filled with regret. If he was the right man for her, wouldn't she have stronger feelings for him? She certainly had very strong feelings for Morgan Murphy, starting with doubt.

She didn't trust Morgan one bit. He raised her hackles, provoked her temper. And he enjoyed doing so. Innis, on the other hand, did everything in his power to make her happy and to see that her dream was realized.

How could she be attracted to two so very different men?

Apparently having been aware of their approach, Mom came back aboard before Cordelia could escape to her cabin. "Did you have a wonderful evening?"

"An interesting one."

Cordelia showed her mother the chain and crescent and explained that she was now partners with Morgan Murphy so the man couldn't simply walk away with the whole mother lode if he found it first.

"Sounds to me like there should be more to that story."

"Wise mother," Cordelia said, kissing her cheek. "I'm off to bed."

Not that she was sleepy.

Back in her cabin, she changed into shorts and a T-shirt, then brought out Elizabeth's journal. Maybe she would read something that would help her figure things out, like how she could be so attracted to a man who was obviously trouble if her wrist burning and ring tightening when she was too close to him was an accurate tell.

Odd, though, that both wrist and ring had been quiet that afternoon when he'd boarded the *Evening Star*.

What in the world could that mean? she wondered as she began to read.

Dunham Castle, 1603

The duke is by my side as I face the man who has betrayed all that we hold dear. The sun streaming in through the narrow windows dapples the cool stone floor with light. It falls upon Carlyle's face, and I see what weapon he will use against me.

I step in front of the duke to protect him, for it is my duty.

"Her child is a bastard as is Stephen. It is to William she gave what should rightfully have been mine."

It is the moment I knew would come. I feel the duke's warmth so close behind me, yet he has not moved, nor have I.

"He was proud of their coupling. He told me so himself in the woods that last day. Ask her if it is not true that she loves only William, and her bastard is his."

Carlyle's triumphant shout swirls around me like an evil net in which I am caught. To deny Will is one blasphemy I will never commit.

I stand tall as I turn to confront the duke.

I see knowledge in his gaze a heartbeat before his mouth moves into a smile. He knows the truth and rejoices.

My heart swells in my breast as I send the silent message he now believes. Nothing else matters except that these are the children of our hearts.

The duke turns to challenge Carlyle, declaring Serena and Stephen to be the children of his body and refusing to deny them.

With hatred in his eyes, Carlyle points his finger at me. "She has bewitched you! She is a witch, and her power lies in her celestial girdle."

Smiling, I uncoil it from my body, sapphire stars and emerald crescent moons twirling from strings of gold and diamonds, and toss it at his feet. I need it no longer, for its power lives within me.

"Take it and be gone."

His expression triumphant, Carlyle picks up the celestial girdle and hugs it to his chest as he leaves, knowing he is banished as the murderer of his brother.

Stephen is now the heir, as I promised Will. His death is in some small measure revenged.

He lives on in me, and in his children. It is for me and for Serena and for Stephen, to think and act always as he would have done.

Remember that the future is for you to write, for it is set firmly in your stars.

It couldn't be!

Cordelia picked up the chain and crescent and remembered the power she'd felt when it had touched her ring and when Morgan had kissed her.

That kiss had been heart-stopping. She'd never experienced a like reaction to any man before—of course it had something to do with the artifact and Elizabeth's magic. This had to be part of Elizabeth's celestial girdle. How had Morgan gotten hold of it?

What did it all mean?

Her birthmark had burned with familiar warning.

According to the journal, Elizabeth had tossed the celestial girdle at the villain Carlyle, who'd taken it with him to his ship. What if he'd passed it down to his descendants the way the keepsake treasure chest and Posey ring had gone through Elizabeth's line?

Dear Lord, what if her mother had been correct when she'd said that if Elizabeth's belief that she and Will would be together again was true, then Carlyle would try to stop them?

Disturbed at the turn the evening had taken, Cordelia slipped the crescent and chain under her pillow and tried to sleep.

Innis held in his emotions until he reached the room in the bowels of *Foley's Treasure*. Once the door was closed and locked, he let out a growl of frustration. Morgan Murphy had some kind of power over Cordelia. If he didn't do something, the pirate would be sure to woo her into his bed.

The thought of Murphy's hands on the woman he loved made his gut clench. Bad enough that Murphy had kissed her.

Worse had been her enthused response.

And then when *he'd* kissed her good night, it hadn't been anything like the kiss they'd shared after he'd saved her from the shark. This time, he'd felt like she had been a million miles away.

Had Murphy filled her thoughts even then?

What to do?

Cordelia was destined to be his. He'd never met another woman that compared to her. She was the love of his life. His soul mate. He couldn't lose her. He would do anything in his power to make Cordelia love him. Brigitte had come up with a love spell and he'd thought why not? He'd been sure Cordelia had just needed a little push. The charm hadn't really worked or the spell had worn off, and Murphy had found a way to steal her interest.

Getting the pirate out of the picture was the key. He had to find a way to discourage Murphy, to give him good reason to leave the dive site. And Cordelia.

And if the pirate wouldn't leave, what then?

He unlocked and opened the doors to Brigitte's closet, to reveal a high, narrow table covered with red velvet, decked with black candles and pots of herbs and vials of oils. Brigitte's domain, kept secret from her husband Leandre, who wouldn't approve of her practicing the black arts of Voodoo rather than the more acceptable, positive religious side.

How humiliating it would be to admit to her that another man had Cordelia's attention after Brigitte had created that fetish for him. Brigitte was expert in all manner of spells and curses, but this was something he didn't want to share with her. He slammed the doors shut.

So how was he going to keep Murphy away from the woman he loved?

Even as Morgan watched the *Evening Star*, he slipped the treasure he'd found in the surf over his ring finger. Surely this had been a wedding ring, a token of love considering the engraving inside the band.

...yet never doubt my love...

His thoughts turned to Cordelia Ward.

He'd only met the lovely and infuriating marine archaeologist that very morning, but oddly enough, it felt to him as if they'd known each other forever. He would have sworn when he held her in his arms to dance that he'd held her before. An electrical current had passed through them when their hands had met with the chain between them. And that kiss...a new experience...more than lust. Never before had he felt so many warring emotions with such little encouragement from a woman.

A challenging woman.

Spirited.

Perhaps more complex than he'd given her credit for.

Cordelia Ward was one to watch. One to get to know better. Assuming she didn't back out of the partnership offer, he would have that chance. If he could only find a way to neutralize Innis Foley's influence over her. Surely that wouldn't be impossible.

With the fireworks simmering between him and Cordelia, if he could keep Innis away from her somehow, it would be no time before he would have her full cooperation on the dive site and in his bed. He would look forward to that.

But tonight he was alone, the memory of her—her scent, her taste, her very peevishness—his only companion.

Undressing and dropping his clothes on the floor, he threw himself into his bunk and clicked off the room light.

Hoping to dream of her.

Chapter Fourteen

The next morning, Cordelia wasn't any more clear about the two men competing for her. The one thing she wasn't at all conflicted over—she had to find the celestial girdle and remove the jeweled dagger from the equation.

Cordelia felt a bump that told her *Foley's Treasure* had been snugged against the *Evening Star*. She heard male voices followed by a thump on the deck above her. Quickly climbing into a swimsuit and oversize T-shirt as a cover-up, she then picked up the artifact Morgan had given her.

The moon and chain had a powerful effect on her, if that dream was any indication. Even now, a thrum from her Posey ring made her think ring and chain "recognized" each other. Not that she would share such a crazy notion with anyone.

But what if having the artifact with her could lead to the more important find?

Hesitating only a second, she pulled the artifact from

under her pillow and hooked the chain together. Then she slipped it over her head, tucking the crescent into the top of her swimsuit, before entering the galley to find her mother entertaining Innis over a cup of coffee.

Wisps of the night's dream still haunting her, she somehow found her voice. "Morning."

Innis's wistful expression made her flush. He wanted her, thought they were destined and longed for her to feel the same. She had no reason to suspect him. Regret coursed through Cordelia. She had no proof that either man was not what he seemed to be. Only the dream cast doubt in her mind. After all his planning for a romantic evening, Innis must have been hurt at the way it had ended, with her distracted by Morgan.

"Sleep well?" he asked.

She flushed. "Don't worry, I'm stoked to dive."

"Great timing." Mom removed a dish from the oven. "Breakfast is ready. Enough for three."

Eggs, bacon, chopped mushrooms, chunks of bread and cheese, all baked together. Cordelia's favorite.

"I don't want to impose, Madelyn."

"You're not imposing." Seeing Innis in person, Cordelia felt the tension from the dream melting away.

Mom insisted. "You need protein before you dive."

Innis shrugged and smiled. "Then I'll have some."

As they ate, they talked about plans for the day.

"I thought you and I should take the first dive with another team," he said.

"Good by me." The sooner she got in the water, the sooner she would have a chance to find the dagger. She simply couldn't put the warning out of mind.

"We'll alternate with the other two teams, then go for a second dive this afternoon."

She asked, "How much of the grid is laid down?"

"Enough to keep us busy for a few days. If we don't find the mother lode within the area, we can expand it."

What if Morgan, staying to the periphery of their work area, had already found the mother lode—the reason he'd had the chain and crescent?

Remembering she'd agreed to his proposed partnership, that she'd agreed to work out the details today, breakfast suddenly lost its taste. She set down her fork and decided talking to the man could wait until after her dive. Fingering the artifact beneath her cover-up, she only hoped it could help her find the knife.

Scraping his own plate clean, Innis gave her mother a nod of approval. "Excellent, Madelyn. Just the right start to the day."

"Delicious," Cordelia agreed, rising and kissing her mother on the cheek.

Taking their plates to the sink, they bumped hips. Cordelia smiled at Innis, who seemed himself again.

"Have a good dive," Mom said, her voice a bit wistful.

Cordelia wanted in the worst way to invite her mother to dive with them, but she suspected it was too soon. Mom had asked her to stop pushing, so she would let things unfold naturally. Not to mention, there was potential danger below the surface if her dream-vision had any validity.

Innis let her cross from the *Evening Star* to *Foley's Treasure* first, but he was right behind her, and he surreptitiously brushed a kiss over her bared shoulder, then winked at her. Warmed by the attention, she smiled at him, then glanced across the yacht to see Morgan's boat lazily bob on the other side, no one on deck.

Had he been so close all night?

At least in her dreams?

Which man?

Checking her gear before donning her wet suit, she tried to put the dream—and her mother's warning about the past catching up to the present—out of mind. But, wanting to know what Morgan was up to, she couldn't help but look for him. The older man, today wearing an oxygen tank that had nothing to do with diving, was now on deck. Was Morgan in the *Sea Rover's* galley, or had he beat them into the water? Was he already investigating the shipwreck?

"Ready?" Innis asked.

"As I'll ever be." Touching the chain and crescent still secured in her swimsuit, hoping again the artifact could lead her to the celestial girdle and therefore the dagger, she zipped up her wet suit.

"Start the magazine," Innis told one of his men.

On the dive platform with a second team, they set their fins, lights, masks, regulators, and mouthpieces in place and rolled back into the water.

As always, the magic of the sea lured Cordelia in deep... deeper...deeper. She wanted to lose herself in the dive. The resurfacing of snippets of the dream prevented that. Too aware of the risk, she darted her gaze in every direction, more focused on preventing the dream from becoming reality than she was on finding the mother lode.

One of the divers found the second cannon, and all three men set about uncovering it. Not that the find was of no interest to her—she was simply distracted.

Though she forced herself to concentrate on visualizing the girdle and dagger, no matter where she looked, no matter how far out she moved on the grid, nothing sparkled at her from within the sands. If the chain and crescent she wore was magically connected to the celestial girdle or any other artifact, it wasn't leading her to them.

So far, they'd only done nonpenetration dives, investigating exterior parts of the wreck easily available. Maybe she needed to go deeper. Maybe the mother lode was still in the bowels of what was left of the old ship.

Glancing over at the other divers, she saw they were focused on their canon and were preparing to bring it up.

Penetrating the light zone of the wreck's structure presented a slightly greater risk, but she would keep the exit point visible, and she did carry a spare light in case the one she was using went out.

Once inside, darkness surrounded her, and she could only see whatever her headlamp lit directly in front of her. She kept an eye out for anything that looked off even as she searched. Useless at this level. She would have to set a line to go deeper, and she wasn't prepared to do so without Innis or one of the other men by her side for safety. She was trained in deep-penetration diving, which meant running a guideline inside the wreck from her starting point. Following a line could be necessary to find her way out if she stirred up sediments.

Thinking she should suggest such a run for that afternoon, Cordelia became alarmed when her wrist suddenly began to burn and her ring tightened in warning. Startled, she looked around to find she wasn't certain of the way out now. Her mind had drifted as she had from the other divers. Making her way through the dark, she hesitated when a plume of sand suddenly surrounded her. Through it, she faintly saw movement straight ahead, but she could make out no other diver.

Sharks?

Gasping at the thought, she nearly panicked, even though no shark appeared. Short of breath, she realized she wasn't getting enough air. Her gauge showed she had nearly half a tank of air left. What the hell?

Trying not to panic—her lungs were already starting to protest—she knew getting to the surface conscious would be a feat. Breathing slowly and shallowly, she reoriented herself and found the exit, then inched upward. Without air, the climb was awkward, and she was feeling unfocused. Her movements became sluggish and off point. Suddenly, from out of nowhere, another diver grabbed onto her and pulled on her mouthpiece. Panicking, she tried fighting until the diver shoved his extra air hose at her.

Gratefully taking it, she sucked in enough air to regain her bearings. Able to breathe again, she relaxed and let him take her up. When they broke the surface, she stared into the man's mask to meet his green-eyed gaze.

Morgan.

The pirate had just saved her life. Grateful, she couldn't help but feel warmth flowing through her. Raising her mask, she said, "Thank you."

"You looked like you were struggling. Like you were out of air. I would have done that for anyone."

She believed him, and the negative feelings she'd had for him suddenly seemed foreign. And irrational. "I was out of air—"

"So what the hell happened down there?" he demanded, pulling up his mask. "Weren't you paying attention to your time?"

Before she could answer Morgan, Innis yelled down from the diver platform. "My God, there you are! I thought you slipped by me and came up. I was just about to go back down to find you."

Indeed, he stood there fully dressed to dive.

The stress of the situation having drained her, she said, "Help me up, would you?"

Innis grabbed her hands, and behind her, Morgan secured her hips and lifted. She was on the platform in seconds.

"I ran out of air!" she gasped.

"Weren't you watching your gauge?" Innis asked as Morgan lunged up beside her.

"According to my gauge, I have half my air left."

Morgan tried to take a look, but, his expression fierce, Innis latched onto the front of his buoyancy-compensator vest and shoved him back against the pilothouse, where he crashed into a slender woman. Thrown off balance, she grabbed Morgan, who kept her from falling.

"Brigitte, are you all right?" Cordelia asked as she struggled with the straps of her vest to remove it.

"No worries," the woman murmured.

Innis helped Cordelia shed her equipment, after which he tested the gauge and tank. He shook his head. "Tank is empty all right. And the gauge is stuck. Either that was some coincidence…or someone tampered with it." He gave Morgan a blazing look.

"Hey, I'm just the Good Samaritan who was trying to help."

That Morgan had been conveniently nearby didn't escape her.

Her good thoughts about him drifted away as the end of the dream replayed itself in full Technicolor in her mind.

Innis glared at Morgan. "You could have swam here in the middle of the night and stolen aboard to do your dirty work."

"Were you trying to stop me from finding the mother lode by scaring me to death?" Cordelia cried.

Morgan's expression went directly to neutral, but his gaze cut through her. "Believe what you will." Not trying to convince her otherwise, he backed up.

She couldn't stop herself from pressing him, from trying to get to the truth. "What happened to the partnership you proposed just last night?"

Was the glory of being the one to find the mother lode so important to the treasure hunter that he was willing to play Russian roulette with her life?

His gaze deepened, and she read things in it she wanted to believe.

"My mistake." He rolled into the water.

Shaking now, she watched him go.

Innis took her in his arms and murmured, "I'll never let him hurt you."

But the suddenly hollow feeling inside her at the way Morgan had closed himself off from her told her that it was already too late.

• • •

All pretense of negotiations gone, Morgan took to the sea like he had a demon inside him. Though he'd been angry just with Innis to start when the man had forced him back, he'd held himself in check for Cordelia's sake. He tried not to think about the ungrateful wretch. He'd helped Cordelia out of a dangerous situation—she could have died down there!—and she'd turned on him in a heartbeat, simply on Foley's say-so. He should have known he couldn't trust her.

Diving alone against all good sense, he was determined to finish his air. He had nearly a third of his tank left. He went deeper than he had before.

His pulse began to thud just visualizing Cordelia, remembering how it felt to hold her in his arms on the dance floor, not to mention the out-and-out chemistry of that kiss. There was more to it, though, a connection he couldn't define. It was as if they had known each other forever, maybe in another lifetime.

Feel it...this need to be together which frightens us both...

Closing his mind to the imagined whisper, Morgan shook himself back to reality.

The kiss meant nothing. He was no sucker. He had to be out for himself—no one else around here gave a damn about him. Well, maybe Emmett. His only regret was that he'd given Cordelia the jeweled chain and moon. Even if he didn't find the celestial girdle, that piece of it would be worth a pretty penny.

Morgan forced his mind to the purpose of the dive. Foley's crew had left the grid, and he took the opportunity to check on what they'd done.

Not much. The sand they'd blown away was already encroaching on the site. Nothing sparkled, nothing so much as shone from the sand. They would have to remove more before finding treasure.

Treasure...*the ring he'd found on the beach*...damn!

He'd forgotten to take it off before diving. Wearing any kind of jewelry in the water was a bad idea. Barracuda especially were drawn by the sparkle. He didn't dare take it off now and put it in a pocket lest he lose it. If he dropped it here, the sand would suck it up and he'd never find it. So on his finger it stayed.

He swam toward an area of the site that peaked his interest, just outside Foley's grid. Sifting through the sand by hand—a soothing, repetitive motion—was good therapy. It calmed the anger seething inside him. He found bits of rusted metal from the ship itself, but nothing of any worth.

And then his ring started feeling too tight. What the hell? Why would his finger suddenly swell? Now that was annoying.

Trying not to let it bother him, Morgan worked for a few minutes more but found nothing to make him want to stay. About to give it up and return to the *Sea Rover*, he realized he wasn't alone. A large shadow was coming straight toward him through the water made murky by the sand he'd disturbed. Certain that it was a shark, he wasn't overly concerned, not until, from the corner of his eye, he caught a glimpse of another shadow arrowing his way. And a third from the other side. The shark wasn't alone. It had friends, and they all seemed too interested in him.

With the damn ring feeling even tighter, he backed off and kicked his flippers, at the same time inflating his BC to bring him more quickly to the surface.

The sharks moved faster.

The three tiger sharks bore down on him, and for the first time in his life while diving, Morgan knew real fear, had to remind himself to keep breathing, to move smoothly, to not give the sharks reason to attack. He slipped his dive knife from the sheath belted to his thigh and prepared to defend himself.

The predators circled him as he rose through the water. The circle grew tighter and tighter, and he could sense them preparing for an attack. Though he could see daylight shimmering overhead, the surface was still some distance away.

And then the biggest of the sharks lunged for him. Without thinking, Morgan struck out, not with his knife hand but with the bared one. He caught the attacker in the nose. The contact ignited something unexpected. A hot, sharp current jolted up through his arm into his teeth and made the shark jerk back.

As if shocked, the predator stopped dead in the water, froze for a few seconds before spinning around. Then like a bullet from a gun, it shot straight away from him.

The other two predators followed suit.

Leaving Morgan limp with relief and more than a little puzzled.

What had just happened?

Still holding the dive knife he hadn't used, he finished his ascent with all senses primed for more trouble.

What the *hell* had just happened?

How had he created what had felt like an electrical shock by hitting the shark in the nose? And he'd drawn his dive knife. Why hadn't he used *that*? It was as if his arm had acted of its own volition. An instinctual move? Or had something...*someone*...prompted it?

Chapter Fifteen

Morgan surfaced and hoisted himself onto the dive platform and just stood there until his world righted itself. His divers were sitting on deck eating lunch. Two were deep in some conversation, the third was listening to music via earphones. Still off-kilter, he removed his mask and flippers.

Coming to the rail, Emmett told him, "Food's on the galley counter," then seemed to take a better look. "Something wrong?"

"I was almost bait for a trio of tiger sharks."

The old man swore and joined him on the dive platform. "Let me help you."

Morgan released the catches of his buoyancy-compensator vest and the first mate relieved him of the weight of the tank.

"What happened down there?" Emmett asked.

As he removed his wet suit, Morgan told him about the scare, leaving out the part about the jolt he'd felt when he smacked the shark in the nose.

"Sounds weird to me. Usually if a diver runs into trouble with a shark, it's because the shark was nearby. But you say these guys came at you out of nowhere?"

Morgan nodded. "Seemed odd to me, too." Then again the whole incident had been odd. He started to gather up his equipment.

"I'll take care of the gear. Go get yourself some chow."

Morgan grunted, boarded the boat, and went below. He was too disturbed by what had happened to feel like eating; nevertheless, he loaded up his plate with beans and chicken. Maybe the sensation of stepping out of his depths would pass.

As he ate, he went over the entire incident in his head and remembered the ring feeling too tight. Not anymore. He pulled it off his finger and stared at it. Ever since he'd found the ring, strange things had been happening to him. He thought about glimpsing the dark-haired woman, about feeling foreign emotions, and hearing voices in his head. About the voice he'd heard on the dive. Had its owner saved him?

Morgan wasn't one to believe in magic.

And yet...

Though it seemed beyond belief, he muttered, "Was it you?"

"Was it who?" Emmett asked, stepping into the galley. "You're talking to that ring you found the other night? What's going on, Morgan?"

Morgan sighed. "I didn't tell you everything. When I smacked the shark, I was wearing this." He indicated the ring.

"And—"

"And this big jolt shot up my arm. It was as if I zapped the shark with a live wire."

"You're saying the power came from the ring?"

He guessed he was because he couldn't think of another explanation. "Crazy, huh?"

"Heard crazier. I've lived around the islands all my life, you know. Lots of superstition. Lots of spells cast, both good and bad. I've seen people with fetishes, mojo bags, Voodoo dolls. And they all worked at times." Emmett sat opposite Morgan and threw what looked like an outline of man cut out in black felt about three inches long. "This is crazy, too."

"What is it?"

"Gris-gris. Found it in one of your vest pockets. Look inside."

Morgan picked up the object made of felt, aware of something hard inside. Widening the opening on one side, he shook out the contents covered with what looked like gunpowder—a small strip of folded paper and a very large tooth.

"Tiger-shark tooth," Emmett muttered.

Morgan started. His first mate had been around these waters all his life, so he would know. Morgan opened the folded paper and sucked in his breath at what was written there: *Morgan Murphy*.

"Looks like someone put a curse on you."

Morgan shook his head but he couldn't deny it, couldn't say he didn't believe it could be possible, not after what he'd just experienced.

"So how did that gris-gris get in your vest pocket?" Emmett asked.

"You got me. Could someone have sneaked onto the *Sea Rover* and planted it during the night?"

"Not without me knowing. I slept on deck last night and I wake up at every little noise. Besides, the sneak would have to know which equipment was yours. Who'd want you to run into trouble anyhow?"

Morgan thought back to what happened right before entering the water. "I saw the Ward woman run out of air and gave her my spare hose. I brought her up and to the salvage boat."

"Saw you bring the woman up…and saw Foley shove you around, too."

"Foley grabbed me by the front of my BC vest to get me away from Cordelia." Morgan replayed the incident in his mind.

"Coulda been him. Or that island woman you banged into."

Morgan couldn't say if one of them had actually done it. "I was angry but also distracted, worried about what happened to Cordelia."

If someone at the dive site had actually used Voodoo against him, Cordelia could be in real trouble.

Innis was glad to be rid of Morgan Murphy. Surely the pirate wouldn't be coming back at Cordelia. Not after an encounter that would scare the living daylights out of any man. Using binoculars, all he'd been able to see were shadowy shapes circling Murphy below.

Watching his second string teams go off the diving platform to continue the search, Innis thought that he'd waited too long for this. Twelve years too long. He and Cordelia never should have been separated. She'd been his from the first moment he'd met her. He'd always known it. This was his opportunity to convince her that destiny had brought them back together after what seemed like an eternity.

If only he'd rescued her before Murphy had. Then he'd be her hero.

"That man," Brigitte said, coming up behind him, "he got some kinda magic of his own."

"What are you talking about?"

"You think them sharks went after him on their own?"

Innis started. "What did you do?"

"I helped you, cher. You want the woman, yes?" Smiling, she shrugged and walked away.

His heart thundered as he stared after her, but he pulled himself together when Madelyn crossed over to *Foley's Treasure*.

Her expression showed her concern. "Innis, what happened?"

A little stunned, he swallowed hard. "Cordelia's air gauge stuck. Don't worry. When we go down again, she'll have a new one."

"I didn't mean that exactly."

"What then?"

"She's upset about something else. I know my daughter. I simply can't get her to open up until she's ready. I thought you might be able to clue me in."

Cordelia had gone over to the *Evening Star*, saying she needed some time alone to think things through.

About him?

"Murphy fed her a line about some partnership last night, then threw it back in her face today."

"Oh." Madelyn's brow drew into a deeper frown. "No wonder she's so upset."

"She's afraid he'll be the one to find the mother lode and then we'll be out in the cold."

"That must be it."

Though Madelyn didn't meet his gaze. Instead she looked over at Murphy's craft as if it could give her the answers she wanted.

Innis's stomach knotted, and he flashed on that kiss he'd seen Murphy force on Cordelia. Surely she couldn't be fooled by that damn pirate. Surely Murphy'd had enough and would be gone for good before he had another chance at her.

Had Morgan messed with her gauge as Innis had hinted? Cordelia had had a moment's doubt about Morgan's intentions, but when she'd seen the vulnerability in his eyes, she hadn't been so certain. Morgan had saved her life. Surely he hadn't put it in jeopardy to play hero.

Pacing the length of her cabin, she wondered why he'd given up so easily. Why he hadn't fought Innis's accusation? She wished that he would have, but his complex nature—his pride—would probably make him do the exact opposite of whatever it was that she wanted.

There was more to Morgan than was apparent. She needed to understand him. In what ways had he been molded by that lifetime of experience her mother had thought was so significant?

If only she knew more about him.

The media loved treasure hunters. Successful ones even more so. She'd seen and read interviews featuring him half-a-dozen times.

How far back did the stories go?

One way to find out. Sitting at her desk, she turned on her laptop and did a search on sunken treasure hunters named Murphy.

The first few pages were links to stories about Morgan over the past decade or so, after he'd set off on his own. She scanned stories about his success bringing up booty in the Caribbean a few years back. Nothing in them revealed any more about the man until she got to an article with a photo of him with his parents, Daniel and Jane Murphy. The older Murphys waxed poetic about their ambitious and talented son, who had just made that valuable find. Apparently the first thing he'd done with the money was to buy a brand-new home for them. The second was to buy a motorcycle for himself.

Having always put her own parents first, Cordelia recognized they had that in common, something she never would have guessed.

Something that made her respect him.

She changed the search to his father. The results on Daniel Murphy took her further and further back in time. Another family photo, parents and three kids, the girl crying in her mother's arms. Morgan must have been sixteen or seventeen. The anger in his expression made him look far older.

The story headline: "Treasure Hunters Lose All."

The article detailed the allegations that multimillionaire Brian Croft had made a handshake deal with the Murphys to find a sunken ship on which he had good information. According to Morgan's father, Croft had promised to pay all equipment and crew expenses. But as it happened, the search for the sunken ship hadn't panned out, and Croft refused to pay the expenses of the failed expedition. Morgan's parents took Croft to court, but since there was no written agreement, it was their word against that of a very wealthy man. Croft claimed that part of the agreement was that the expenses were to have been paid from the treasure, but since there was no treasure, his obligation was done. The Murphys claimed that stipulation had never been brought up. The judge ruled in favor of Croft.

Morgan and his family lost their home and were left destitute.

Obviously, a man as wealthy as Brian Croft could have afforded to pay for the expedition no matter the outcome. It was obvious to Cordelia that he chose to financially ruin a family because he didn't get what he wanted.

Sorrow filled her.

No wonder Morgan had bought his parents that new home.

No wonder Morgan had such an attitude.

This business had devastated Morgan's family, and yet he continued working it, albeit in such an aggressive, coercing way. He obviously had a softer side, but he wouldn't let anyone see it. Because he feared that someone might victimize *him*?

Did he think *she* would do so?

Certain that it was doubtful she would find information closer to the bone about Morgan than that, Cordelia sat back in her chair and closed the lid on the laptop.

Had she been unfair to him earlier, questioning him about his intentions? Maybe. She knew Innis didn't like Morgan, undoubtedly the reason he held the treasure hunter suspect. But there had been no proof that anyone had tampered with her equipment. The gauge sticking may have been nothing more than inexplicable bad luck. Morgan had walked away rather than having to justify himself.

She couldn't leave things like that between them.

She wouldn't be Morgan's Brian Croft.

Facing Morgan might be uncomfortable, but it was necessary. She would do so the next day. He'd made her an honest offer of partnership, and though he'd pressured her into accepting, she felt honor-bound to at least talk to him about it, even if the idea made her uncomfortable. She would have a difficult time keeping on track when the man in question could so easily distract her.

No other man had ever made her feel so truly alive. So thoroughly connected when they'd kissed.

She tried convincing herself it had been the chain between their hands that had electrified her. The treasure itself had seduced her.

So why didn't she believe it?

Chapter Sixteen

Morgan spent the evening going over his maps, over his plans for the next day. He had a difficult time concentrating. He kept seeing Cordelia underwater struggling for air, kept wondering what had truly happened to her air gauge. He had to stop this. Worrying about her served no purpose. He needed to focus since, obviously, he would be on his own as always. No way would Cordelia want to have anything to do with him, not after today.

That didn't keep him from worrying. Or from wanting.

He steeled himself against what he couldn't have. And concentrated on what he could.

What he'd wanted for years was to find a mother lode that would enhance his reputation as a treasure hunter. He had to keep his goals in mind. He *would* succeed. He would make his parents proud of him, of themselves, make them stop feeling like failures because they had never gotten rich off of the sea. They were the ones who'd instilled the love of this life in him. They were the ones who'd taught him his trade.

Rising from his desk, he stared out the porthole at the *Evening Star*. Cordelia Ward was his competition. He would beat her. And then maybe he would seduce her.

But not tonight.

Tonight, dreaming of having her would have to be enough. For now.

Will lifts her high in his arms to watch the glorious play of starlight in her wide eyes. "I want to wake each morning with your back curled into me and my hands on your body. Please come with me, Elizabeth."

Morgan tossed and half woke, murmuring, "Cordy?" but the erotic dream pulled him in deeper.

Her breast crushed against his bare chest, he feels each beat of her heart as he carries her from the warm pool to the soft, flower-rimmed earth.

Her half smile is warm without hesitation, her fingers swift drawing the last of his clothes from his body and letting her dress pool at her feet.

The slope of her shoulders, the high, rounded mounds of her breasts with their tight, small nipples, the gentle swell of her hips fill him with the fierce need to worship every part of her.

Their gazes find each other, his mouth hovering over hers.

"Yes, Will. I want to lie with you always." Her whisper is a sweet breath on his lips.

Touching his fingertips along her throat, he feels her tremble and the joy of loving her overflows every sense. "Love, I promise we shall find paradise together."

Waking with a start in the vague space between midnight and dawn, Morgan felt his pulse beat in his throat. Satisfaction in his groin. A yearning he didn't understand.

He'd seen her again. The dark-haired woman. Only this time she had been with a man.

She had been with *him*.

Somehow...

A dream. Of course it had been a dream. It hadn't been real. Hadn't been a memory.

It had just seemed so...

He'd felt so...

Consumed.

But consumed by Cordelia. His night companion might have had dark hair but he'd *felt* Cordelia.

He slipped his hand down his shaft. He was hard. Ready for her again.

Remembering their electric kiss, he closed his eyes and willed Cordelia to come to him.

Again.

"Will, follow me into Paradise."

The warm water of the spring fed pool tugs at Elizabeth's gown as she urges Will to follow her.

He holds her face between his palms, and she comes alive under his touch, the world brightening and pulsing before her eyes.

Gently, he lays his lips on hers, then draws away.

His eyes drifting half closed, his clever fingers part her lips, his mouth returning to hers again. The pounding sweetness of his kiss makes her whimper with physical desire.

He slips his hands down until they cup her buttocks and lift her closer to him. The folds of her gown separating them could not quell her instinctive need to be seamlessly a part of him.

Here.

Now.

Under this moon.

Beneath these stars...

"Elizabeth?" Cordelia murmured, only half-awake.

She'd never dreamed of Elizabeth and Will before... not like this.

Yearning to find them once more, she gave over to her dreamland.

Their nude bodies slick with water float gently beneath the surface.

He hovers over her, his pale flesh so lovely and irresistible in the faint light of the waning moon.

How has she done without him all this time?

How has she done without the kisses he laves over her body? Without the touches so soft and seductive?

He thumbs her nipples, and she arches toward him, urging him to take her in his mouth. He captures her, and she melts in the warm cavity, her nipple alternately softening and then hardening to a turgid peak.

Sweeping around her face by the current, her hair keeps her from really seeing him with her eyes. But no matter, she recognizes him, for she can see with her soul.

Her soul knows him.

Knows they are meant to be.

Knows they are one.

He slides down her body like fluid, his mouth exploring every rib, every curve. She tangles her fingers in his hair as he parts her thighs to taste her. His tongue is clever, makes her pant, makes her swallow seawater.

Gasping out a stream of air bubbles, she widens her thighs for more.

He slips in a finger. A second. A third. All the while, he teases her center with his tongue. Her hips lift in supplication. She is so close to the edge, but this will not do. She tears at his shoulders until he releases his grip on her and floats up. The tendrils of her hair tie them together as his mouth covers hers.

A kiss as deep as the sea.

They sink to the ocean's floor, her only thought to make them one. She reaches down for him, grasps his length, pleasures herself by pulling on the foreskin so it slides over the tip, making him groan into her mouth. She guides him to her, her inner flesh quivering with heated anticipation.

Sand scrapes her spine and comes alive, as tendrils of sparkling chain snake upward, followed by a jewel-encrusted golden mesh that wraps around her waist.

The celestial girdle!

He slides his palms around the girdle and pulls her so close she can hardly breathe. The chains wrap around his back and tighten, binding them together. Every inch of her flesh comes alive in a way she'd never before experienced. Through the depths, she sees a star shoot overhead as he enters her, their hands twined together, rings connecting like a thunderbolt.

Doubt the stars are fire, yet never doubt my love…

As his pulsing rhythm fills her, she cries out. The celestial girdle lifts them from their own bodies, spiraling through the heavens… higher and higher…at last where they belong. Together.

Lightning strikes all around them.

Thunder rumbles approval.

And for a moment, she is lit from within, knowing at last a perfect balance of desire and love.

Then suddenly—unexpectedly—the girdle releases them and falls away, and they plunge back down through the skies and back into the water where they split apart.

Shocked, she tries to get back to him, but now dressed in diving gear, he remains just out of reach, hurtling ahead, racing toward the glow of jewels as the girdle returns to its hiding place in the wreck.

Her wrist burns...her ring tightens...

As she realizes he is reaching for the treasure...Her heart misses a beat when another hand beats him to it, freeing a bejeweled gold dagger from the girdle and flashing the sharp blade toward his air hose...

Awakening in the middle of the night, her wrist burning, her ring too tight, Cordelia was unsettled. No dream had ever been so real to her or had ever felt so right...

Elizabeth and Will...she had recognized their love in a way she never had before...and then the dream had shifted...as if her soul had actually recognized and claimed another's, just as Elizabeth's had claimed Will's.

But whose?

She'd never seen his face.

Had it been Innis? Or Morgan?

The night vision had ended with one man trying to kill the other after removing the dagger from the girdle. At least now she knew it was connected with what Carlyle believed to be the source of Elizabeth's magic.

Was one of them really willing to kill for the treasure?

Literally?

Which man?

Morgan was the pirate. Would he do anything to get what he wanted?

Then, why give her the chain and crescent from the celestial girdle? To trick her into trusting him?

Or was she taking her dream-vision too literally?

Chapter Seventeen

"Aren't you going down with us?" Innis asked Cordelia the next morning as his crew prepared for their first dive of the day.

"Not this morning. After yesterday…well, I need to recover." She was hedging and hoping he believed her. "We'll see how I feel later."

All an excuse to buy her enough time to do what she needed to.

Innis put his arms around her and hugged her. "I'm just glad you're safe. Take what time you need. You'll know when you're ready."

Her mother came out of the galley as Cordelia said, "Thanks for being so understanding."

Brushing his mouth lightly over hers, Innis stepped back. Cordelia smiled at him and waved him off.

"What's going on?" her mother asked. "You've had scares before. It's not like you to let one stop you from diving."

Cordelia kept her voice low. "I'm not letting it stop me. There's something important I have to take care of first."

"Are you going to tell me about it?"

"I need to talk to Morgan." And knowing Innis wouldn't like it, she hadn't wanted to tell him the truth. "You were right about him."

Her mother accepted that explanation without insisting on more.

Seeing men gathering on the dive platform of the *Sea Rover*, Cordelia picked up her binoculars and looked for Morgan, but he was not among the three divers there. She spotted him on deck with the older man. Good. Innis was just taking his team down to the wreck. She waited until they disappeared below the surface and then lowered the dinghy.

"Good luck," Mom said.

Cordelia gave her a thumbs-up and took the dive ladder down to the small boat. She locked the oars in position and rowed toward the *Sea Rover*. By the time she got close, the three divers had already started their descent. She tied up and scrambled onto the dive platform.

Morgan was waiting for her at the rail. He didn't say a word, rather gave her a burning look before turning away. Her pulse threaded unevenly as she stepped up onto his boat. He'd disappeared, as had the old man. She stood on deck for a moment, before going into the galley. Morgan was there. Alone.

Leaning on a counter, he stood, arms crossed over his chest, staring at the door as she came in.

Waiting for her.

She swallowed hard. Just seeing him standing there looking so arrogant and judgmental made her stomach knot.

"We need to talk, Morgan."

"Why? So you can accuse me of something else? I'm done playing nice, Cordelia, so you should be very careful."

He'd called her Cordelia rather than Cordy. Of course he was still angry. Done playing nice? When had he started?

She kept her temper in check. She was here to learn the truth.

"I was so upset at running out of air yesterday, I—I didn't know what to think," she told him with complete honesty.

"So you let Foley do the thinking for you."

"I'm sorry." She really was. "But I've had time to think on my own now. It occurred to me…why would you save me if you had tampered with my gauge so that I would run out of air?"

"Maybe I set it up so I could play hero."

She'd considered that, but she didn't believe him. "Why?"

"Isn't it obvious?"

He pushed away from the counter and came at her.

Her mouth went dry and her heart started to thud, but she held her ground.

He stopped mere inches from her, but she felt as if his energy was pulling her closer until only a hairbreadth separated them.

"Why are you really here, Cordy?"

So it was Cordy again. She forced a smile. "The partnership…I thought you wanted that."

Sliding a hand behind her neck, he said, "This is what I want," as he pulled her to him and covered her mouth with his.

She gave herself over to the kiss.

Lost herself in the moment.

Opened herself to feelings that she rarely acknowledged.

Need drew her arms up around his neck and she pressed herself harder against him. Want hazed her mind and opened her to his touch. Desire made her want more, everything he could give.

Until seductive whispers from somewhere froze her...

You have imprinted your soul on mine...for eternity...

...as you have on mine...our destiny...

Cordelia pulled her head free but couldn't push herself away from Morgan. Her lips centimeters from his, she whispered, "Did you hear that?"

He didn't answer. Didn't move. Didn't press her.

Had he heard? Why didn't he say something?

Why couldn't he be honest with her? She was trying...

Trembling, she pulled away from him. Their gazes locked in a mental embrace that felt like it could go on forever.

Until uncertainty forced her to break the connection and ask, "Why did you back out on being partners with me?"

"I want *you*, Cordy, but not with Foley along for the ride."

Which sounded like he wanted *her* more than a business partnership. All right, so that was honest.

Her pulse raced as she said, "Innis is not just along for the ride. I hired him and gave him a stake in the find because he's the best at what he does."

"And because you have a soft spot for him?"

"What if I do? He means something to me." Old feelings for Innis had resurrected over the past few days, but she now realized they were just that—memories.

"So you're blinded by the past."

Cordelia shook her head. "I don't know what that's supposed to mean."

"That you don't know Foley anymore. You don't know the kind of man he is now or what he's done to get where he is. You're not paying attention, Cordy."

The haze in her mind cleared. "I'm paying attention now, Morgan. What exactly are you saying?"

"If someone tampered with your gauge, then who would have better reason?"

He still hadn't said that he *hadn't* done it.

"You're accusing *Innis* of trying to kill me?"

"Or of playing a very dangerous game in trying to win you back from me."

"Who said you had me?"

"Your being here says it for you."

Mentally pulling away, Cordelia felt enveloped by a chill she couldn't shake. Morgan was so sure of himself. Innis had accused Morgan of tampering with her gauge and now Morgan was accusing Innis. Which man was telling the truth? How was she to know?

As if he could read her, Morgan said, "You have to make up your mind, Cordy. You have to decide who you should trust. You wear your uncertainty like a suit of armor to protect you. You need to decide," he said again. "Only *you* can decide what is true."

Cordelia backed away from him.

Morgan didn't try to stop her.

Making her way back to the *Evening Star* as fast as she could row, Cordelia felt crushed under the weight of that armor Morgan spoke of and wondered how to rid herself of it for once and for all.

• • •

For once and for all, Innis had to rid himself of Morgan Murphy.

The pirate had conquered the gris-gris that Brigitte had admitted to planting on Murphy. Surely she could come up with something more efficient, the reason he'd had Brigitte meet him.

She took one look at the open altar, at the lit candles and incense and seemed pleased with herself. Innis clenched his jaw. This wasn't the way he normally did things, but he was desperate. He wasn't going to let that pirate steal what was his. He would do what he had to, just as he had when he'd wrested the salvage company from his father.

As if she knew that, Brigitte's lips curled in satisfaction. "What is it you want me to do this time?"

"To secure my destiny—both Cordelia and bringing up the mother lode of the *Celestine*. It was my ancestor who lost it during a hurricane. And it was during another hurricane that I found myself."

She seemed puzzled at that. "You are speaking in circles."

"Then let me explain. Twelve years ago, Foley Salvage partnered with the Wards to bring up the mother lode of *De Oro Del Casco*. That's when I met Cordelia. From that first moment, I felt the connection. Very soon I became aware—"

"That you loved her."

"That was part of it. There was more." He would tell her all so she would understand what he'd known all these years. "When the winds picked up, announcing the arrival of the hurricane, everything intensified. Every time I touched Cordelia, I got glimpses into another world. The past. I suddenly *knew* Cordelia on a level I couldn't explain. I became obsessed with her even as the hurricane struck full force. Unfortunately, the storm destroyed the dive site and her parents gave up. They took her from me, and our paths didn't cross again until a few years ago. But the connection, the obsession, remained...never to be forgotten throughout the years."

"So you knew each other in another lifetime. Souls who know each other never forget."

"I want to know Cordelia, to *have* her, in *this* lifetime, and Morgan Murphy stands in my way. He needs to be gone."

She murmured, "You need something from your past life when you and she were first together..."

"I don't understand."

"That's where your power lies," Brigitte said. "In the past."

"In what exactly?"

"This is for you to learn. You must be willing to give yourself over to the loa Agwe. He will guide your hand."

If a Voodoo god could help him, so be it. "Whatever it takes."

Brigitte nodded and stepped to the altar, Innis following, his intent to watch her every move. There she mixed several powders and chips in a mortar and used the pestle to grind them together, all the while whispering to the loa in an island *patois* Innis vainly tried to follow. Then she scrawled the names *Innis Foley, Cordelia Ward*, and *Morgan Murphy* on a piece of parchment, which she rolled up before setting the end into the black candle's flame. The parchment flared for a moment and smoked. The material burned fast, and as it crumbled, the ash fell into the mortar, where she mixed it into the powder.

When she was done, Brigitte turned to Innis. "You must

now close your eyes and open your mind."

Nodding, Innis did as demanded as she began her plea to the loa.

"Oh, Agwe, god of the sea, ruler of all below the water's surface, lord of the underworld, ferrying dead souls and keeping watch over the oceans. Enter Innis Foley so that you can guide him back into his past where he first met his woman. Allow him to see what he must to rid himself of the obstacle to his desires for both her and the treasure you hold in your watery arms."

Innis heard her take a breath and blow…felt fine powder spray over his face and neck…His body jerked, his mind trying to tear away from him. Instinct made him fight to keep control, but it was a losing battle.

"Submit…" Brigitte insisted "…and let Agwe enter and guide you…"

He jerked again. And again. No control. Not over his body nor over his mind.

"*Submit if you wish to overcome your obstacle,*" came her whisper, which now seemed hollow and very far away.

Submit…

Eyes still shut tight, Innis relinquished control and his body rolled and jerked and moved without his knowing how. A deep, guttural sound escaped him. His mind was on fire, hurtling backward through decades and then through centuries.

Suddenly, he saw her in his mind's eye…Cordelia and not Cordelia…dark hair…green eyes…but her. She was wearing the celestial girdle. And she was with him.

"*Joined with me I shall release your full dark power,*" he says. "*Together we shall conquer time and space.*"

"Never!" She pulls a jeweled gold dagger from her girdle and aims it at his heart.

He laughs. "Good. You like your play rough. As do I." He lunges toward her.

Some force like unseen hands flings him back away from her.

Then she hadn't loved him, after all!

Anger made him try to pull away from the force controlling him, but determination made him give back over. Perhaps she hadn't been his in a previous life, but she *would* be his in this one.

"Agwe, show me what I must do," he growled, and his mind immediately whirled forward in time and then stopped deep beneath the water's surface.

He allows Agwe to pull him where the loa will, faster and faster toward the depths of the ocean's floor. Then suddenly Agwe frees him, and he hangs suspended over what looks like a dark shadow.

The darkness takes shape—the hulk of the Celestine.

Elated, he skims along the rotting bones of the once-powerful British galleon, now scattered along the seafloor. Centuries have spread the remains...and another diver has beaten him to it.

Even as the other diver reaches for treasure, he shoots forward, his hand driving into the sand-covered mother lode and finding the handle of a dagger.

Pulling it free of the sand, he strikes out...

Sucking in a huge breath, Innis opened his eyes and met Brigitte's gaze. A slow, knowing smile curled her lips.

"Now you know what you must do to get what you want."

Chapter Eighteen

Dunham Castle, 1605

    Last night in my dream flight I hovered above the vortex of wind in which Carlyle's ship floundered. The monstrous waves crashed into the wooden hull as the screaming wind ripped the sails to shreds.

    Carlyle gave no thought for the woman and child but only sought to keep safe his treasure. The wooden chests filled with silver, gold, and jewels. The five hundred heavy bars of gold. Ingots of silver, rubies, emerald, diamonds, and pearls by the hundreds. The heavy pieces of jewelry set with precious stones. All sinking to the bottom of the sea.

    He saw that I was there as I promised and he gave a silent scream as he drowned, entangled within my celestial girdle beneath the warm waters, which wash the shores of the New World.

    I saw the woman and the boy she calls his son reach land safely. They will bother Serena and Stephen no more from that far off place.

    Yet their role in the play is not finished.

    At last the curtain of time has parted to show me a glimpse of the final act.

The part of me which never dies will find Will at last. Know that if I combed the earth and searched through the galaxies for eternity there is no being I would want but this one. And so it shall be when once again passion beats between us like a living force.

I long for this with every breath I draw. Yet I have foreseen that once again Carlyle's evil shall rip us asunder.

Do not be so bewitched by enchantment that you believe all danger is past.

For you and I are one.

Feeling as if she'd just seen the *Celestine* sink through Elizabeth's eyes—a supernatural feat on her ancestress's part that took away her breath—Cordelia set down the journal in the middle of her bunk. Her own abilities of having precognitive dreams and a brush with telekinesis were dwarfed by comparison.

Elizabeth had written: *That future is for you to write for it is set firm in your stars.* And: *For you and I are one.*

Had Elizabeth meant her specifically? Was she the *"you"* in the journal? Was she meant to fulfill Elizabeth's destiny and find her Will?

Or was it the Will, as in Will reincarnated?

Was she Elizabeth reborn?

All along, the journal had drawn her closer and closer to the past. The dreams had taken her to another level, had shown her what she now believed to be true.

At first she'd been afraid to believe.

Never having known that kind of love, she hadn't been open to it.

But that last dream had convinced her, had seduced her in new ways. She wanted its promise. Needed it. And only one man could give it to her.

Which man? she wondered, hoping it would be the one who had her heart.

Open your mind and you will know what is true…

Had she really heard a woman's voice? "Elizabeth?"

No answer.

So, closing her eyes, Cordelia went through every moment of the past days.

Innis saving her from the shark. Morgan giving her his spare air hose.

Innis romancing her. Morgan trying to seduce her.

Innis doing all in his power to make her dreams real. Morgan trying to take them from her.

She concentrated on finding the truth. She needed to know for certain who to trust. Her hand went to the chain still around her neck. She fingered its length, and the moment the ring and crescent met, a charge of power shot through her entire body.

Her wrist burned.

The ring tightened.

Her mind opened.

Though she was awake this time, a dream-vision threw her back to the underwater realm.

The diver hurtles through the water, racing toward the wreck.

Which man? she thinks frantically, needing to uncover his identity now, before it is too late.

He plunges inside the maw, and without hesitation, continues straight into the bowls, his headlamp the only light…

Horrified, she realizes he is making a deep penetration.

Her wrist and her ring set off like a fire alarm…

A deep penetration without his first setting a line puts him in serious danger.

What is he thinking? What if he can't find his way back out?

Another danger follows. She senses more than sees a school of tiger sharks.

Her breath catches in her throat and the flesh along her spine raises. No way to warn him as the danger multiplies.

Another diver follows the sharks. The man who would kill him.

Which man?

She thinks she knows but she has to be certain.

The events of the past days race through her mind. Every word, every action, every look...

Jerked out of the vision, Cordelia shook with dread.

One man would be a victim, the other a killer, unless she stopped it from happening.

"No, Morgan, don't do it!" she cried, rushing from her cabin straight through the galley and across the deck past her mother reading in a lounge chair.

"Cordelia?"

"Later, Mom."

She jumped to the salvage ship.

Two of the divers leaned against the rail of *Foley's Treasure.* Chatting, they stopped when she stepped down from the rail.

"Innis—where is he?" she asked, rubbing at her birthmark. It wouldn't quiet.

One of the men said, "He's already below."

That's what she'd been afraid of. She looked to the *Sea Rover* on the other side of the *Evening Star.* The man with the oxygen tank had his feet propped on the ledge. To her horror, he was smoking.

"Where's Morgan?" she yelled.

The man's wrinkled face pulled into a grin. He pointed to the water. "Waiting for you to join him."

Certain Morgan had said no such thing, Cordelia ignored the wet suit, and the protection it offered. Getting below quickly was critical, so she pulled a harness over her swimsuit and secured it in record time. Her wrist was on fire and growing hotter and more insistent, and her ring threatened to cut off her finger.

Birthmark and ring had acted up every time Morgan was around Innis, not because he was dangerous, but because he was the one in danger. Considering both were activated without his presence, she knew her dream vision was about to be realized if she didn't stop it.

"Help me!" she ordered the divers.

They jumped up. One grabbed a fresh tank, while the other gathered the peripherals.

"The gauge is new," the first said, attaching the tank to her back. "I checked it out myself."

The other one said, "Hey, you want to leave that here?" He was pointing to the chain around her neck.

"No."

Sticking the crescent back into the top of her swimsuit, Cordelia hoped it could somehow help her save Morgan. She jumped down to the dive platform, pulled on her fins and mask, then checked her regulator and clamped down on the mouthpiece even as she rolled herself into the sea. Praying she wasn't too late to save the man she should have recognized as her soul mate, the one meant to share her life as Will should have shared his with Elizabeth.

She wouldn't let it happen.

Not again.

Elizabeth hadn't been able to save Will.

Cordelia wouldn't let Morgan die.

Chapter Nineteen

Below her, a diver skimmed the hulk of the wreck, his light catching the opening to penetrate it. Cordelia did a three-sixty twirl to scan the area, but she didn't see a second diver.

Was one of them already exploring inside?

Turning back to the wreck, she realized she was alone. The diver she'd seen had disappeared. She forgot to breathe for a second, and her heart began to pound. Her wrist was burning off the charts and the Posey ring had tightened until her forefinger had gone numb.

Elizabeth, help me be as fearless as you…

She shot toward the dark maw of the wreck, her bare flesh raising when a cold current caught her. The discomfort wouldn't stop her. Nothing could.

She noted no line as she entered. She'd been so panicked to stop a murder that she hadn't brought one herself. Hesitating a second, trying to figure out what to do, she started when a woman's voice whispered through her mind…

Save him, and I will guide you both back to safety.

Elizabeth?

Had she really heard that, or was her imagination working overtime?

Whichever, Cordelia had to believe that she could save Morgan and get them back out of the wreck. What would happen after that wasn't clear.

First things first.

Lights ahead guided her. There was some distance between the two headlamp beams and both stayed focused straight ahead. Was Innis following Morgan and Morgan didn't know it? Although she'd had feelings for Innis, in her heart, she believed in Morgan. She trusted the connection between them that had become so evident to her. Something fast and sleek cut within the fading beam of Innis's light, and Cordelia knew it to be a shark. Swallowing hard, she had to put it out of mind to go on.

Instead she thought about Innis, who'd won her young heart for a season, who had played the good friend for years.

How could she have been so mistaken about him?

My greatest enemy, Carlyle, wielded the deadly dagger, yet I must marry him.

Elizabeth's journal haunted her.

I will act well my role in this play.

Then when the moment is right, I shall step to the edge of the stage between the light and the darkness beyond. From this place, hidden yet exposed, I will claim what is right and just for those I love.

As she would do, Cordelia vowed.

If her role was Elizabeth and Morgan was her Will, then Innis had to be Carlyle.

Cordelia knew Innis hated Morgan, but enough to kill him? There had to be more to this horror. Surely not her. Surely this couldn't be jealousy that drove him.

Even as she thought it, she knew it was part of the truth. Innis wanted her. Plus he wanted the glory that went with finding the mother lode, not to mention his portion of the treasure's worth.

They were all guilty of wanting the glory. All three of them.

She'd wanted the glory of the find enough to close her heart against Morgan when he'd tried to win her over. All the things she'd thought about him were true of herself. Though she might have wanted to pump the will to live back into her mother, she'd also wanted the fame of the find to assure her own reputation as a marine archaeologist. So she'd viewed Morgan with distrust and had let that stop her from really knowing him, really seeing through the veil of suspicion Innis had created.

She'd fought her feelings for Morgan until that moment he'd given her his spare airline and had brought her up to safety. She'd softened to him then, only to allow Innis to twist her mind against Morgan yet again when he hadn't deserved it. And then for those few seconds before he'd escaped back to the sea, she'd seen the truth in Morgan's eyes.

Pulling out of her thoughts, Cordelia realized the first headlamp had stopped moving and the second had gone out. Her pulse roared, and for a moment she couldn't catch her breath.

Innis...where was he?

Undoubtedly, he'd turned off his lamp to make a stealth approach.

Hoping Innis hadn't already seen her, Cordelia clicked off her own headlamp and arrowed straight for Morgan's light. A hard, sleek body slithered against her arm, jerking her to the side, and her heart nearly jumped from her chest.

Tiger shark!

She froze.

They are not your enemy. Trust yourself.

Taking a shallow, ragged breath, Cordelia listened to the voice in her head and swam straight toward the man she'd mistakenly mistrusted.

Morgan's beam picked up a brilliant gleam in the sand below him—emeralds set in a crescent of gold. Her pulse picked up a beat. He waved the sand from the artifact and revealed a patch of gold mesh. When he pulled at it, Cordelia could see that he'd found Elizabeth's celestial girdle, and as he fought to pull it free, other, smaller treasures popped out of the sand.

He'd found the mother lode.

She shot toward Morgan faster.

Then another headlamp clicked on, taking Morgan's attention from the treasure.

Innis reached past him and from the girdle still half-buried in a sandy grave, removed the dagger.

A frantic Cordelia closed the distance between them, and as Innis raised the blade to strike, she grabbed his hand to stop him. His gaze met hers through their masks. She saw surprise and then the shock of betrayal. They struggled for control of the dagger. The blade nicked his thigh. He jerked hard and pulled free of her grip.

Before he could strike out again, Morgan lunged upward and shoved Innis away from her. A thin trail of blood from

Innis's thigh wound followed.

Innis came back at Morgan and the men struggled in bizarre silence. Just when Cordelia feared the dagger would find its way to Morgan's heart, he knocked Innis's arm hard. The dagger dropped back to the sea's floor.

Morgan moved toward Cordelia, and a current sizzled between them even before he reached her. She felt as if she was just seeing the real man now for the first time. Her heart pulsed with anticipation. He held out his hand to her, and she took it. The touch was electric, a pulse that beat throughout her, and she realized he was wearing the Posey ring that was mate to hers.

Before he could draw her away from further danger, she saw Innis recover the dagger. He came at them, blade raised to pierce Morgan's back. Cordelia shoved her love out of the way.

The dagger struck...

...her...

...plunging hilt-deep into her stomach.

Shocked by the pain, Cordelia froze, saw her life's blood ooze from the wound in dark, foggy fingers swirling around her, saw Innis before her, his eyes behind the mask opening wide in horror.

Movement from the corner of her eye raised the flesh along her spine. Drawn by the scent of blood, the sharks were circling, motions increasingly frantic.

Clasping her hands around the dagger hilt, fearing to free it and do more damage, she tried to stem the blood with her fingers.

Morgan reached for the chain and crescent. No sooner had he lifted the artifact over her head than Innis grabbed him around the neck from behind and ripped his air hose from his mouth. Apparently Innis had vanquished any regret. He closed both hands around Morgan's neck and squeezed. Morgan struggled, but without air didn't have what he needed to free himself.

Growing weaker from each second of blood loss, Cordelia despaired. She could do nothing to save Morgan. She could do nothing to save herself. She could barely move. They were both going to die.

Don't give up. Born on Witches' Night, we are magic. Use our power...

Cordelia tried to focus on the words whispered in her mind.

Power.

Elizabeth's power.

Their power.

The sharks were closing in on them, drawn by the blood billowing from her wound and from the cut on Innis's thigh. Soon they would grow bold enough to attack.

Cordelia focused her mind on finding some way out of this. The girdle! She switched on her headlamp to look for it, but the seafloor had claimed it once more. Picturing the priceless artifact, she called to it with her mind. She visualized it—every gem-studded detail—and directed her thoughts to lifting the girdle from its watery grave. Within seconds, bejeweled strands of chain snaked out from their briny hiding place.

Concentrating with everything she had, Cordelia called on her latent telekinesis. Emotions high, she urged the source of Elizabeth's power from its grave inch by inch, at the same time visualizing what she wanted of it.

Suddenly, the girdle seemed to take on a life of its own and flew at the would-be murderer. It wrapped around his back and Innis jerked and let go of Morgan, who quickly recovered his air hose. The girdle's chains snaked around Innis and held him captive, suspended and unable to flee, no matter that he fought it with fury.

Morgan kicked him away and swam to her side, pulling her from the path of the sharks closing in. When one came too close, he snapped the chain still in his hand and smacked the predator in the nose with the crescent. Sparks shot where it hit, and the shark swam off into the deep.

Mere yards from them, Innis fought to free himself from the threat of several sharks working up to attack, but Elizabeth's magic held him fast.

Cordelia's vision dimmed. Morgan was alive. She'd fought the dream-vision and won this time. She might be lost, but at least he was saved. She would have the comfort of his arms around her as she joined Elizabeth in her celestial home.

Her eyes grew heavy, her head light. She felt disembodied. *Dying.*

Suddenly her life flashed before her, from the kiss with Morgan at the club backward...back to the hurricane the summer a dozen years before when she'd met Innis...and further yet...

She threw herself onto Will's hard chest, and his powerful arms closed around her. "To have had such a love"—she sobbed, swallowing tears—"and to have lost it is a tragedy of the soul." She flung back her head, resting it on his shoulder, and gazed up at him. "In God's eyes, you are the duke's firstborn son. I should be yours."

Excruciating pain slid through Cordelia as the dagger slid out of her side. Her eyes fluttered open for a last look at Morgan before she died. She could feel more than see his panic.

We have become one in all ways.

We have pledged our love with Posey rings which will last for eternity. And so we will confess to the duke who I know will bless our love.

In joy I have made my choice.

Yet in this moment my joy is turning to fear.

Something cold and hard pressed against her flesh. Forcing herself to focus, Cordelia saw that Morgan had placed the crescent from the girdle over the wound.

Again I feel the terror of finding Will fallen upon the grass, blood gushing from his wounds, staining red the earth beneath him.

Again feel my joy when I press a crescent from my celestial girdle against his flesh and it heals into a scar of the waxing moon upon his wrist as it did on Laurel's forehead.

Again the blackness consumes me as the powers of my celestial girdle are not great enough to heal the deep stab wound in Will's back...

Morgan was trying to save her the same way Elizabeth had tried to save Will, Cordelia realized.

Too late for Will...too late for her...

Behind her mask, she wept, for finally she understood what Elizabeth had meant when she'd written

...we are one and shall meet and fight for what is written in our stars.

Through the veil of time I have seen the face of you who comes after me, and I have seen Carlyle beside you. He shall menace you with his evil. You must defy him and overcome his magic curse.

Believe this, for it will be true for you.

Cordelia touched Morgan's face and looked into emerald-green eyes that spoke the truth, just as they had when she'd accused him of tampering with her air gauge. She'd recognized hurt then, and now the hurt, more desperate, dug deeper. Despite the fact that she'd given him absolutely no reason, Morgan cared for her.

Beyond him, the sea thrashed red with fury.

Horrified, she realized the boy she had once loved was finished. He'd been finished the moment he'd put his plan to get rid of Morgan into action. She didn't even know the man he'd become. Even so, digging her fingers into Morgan's arms to brace herself, she couldn't help the tears gathering inside her mask.

As the sharks tore Innis to pieces, Morgan forced her upward so she didn't have to watch.

Chapter Twenty

Morgan willed Cordelia to live, and by the time he got her back to the surface a short swim from the boats, her bleeding had stopped. A voice in his head had made him press the crescent around her wound. Underwater, he felt as if another had controlled him to save Cordelia. Now he replaced the chain and crescent around her neck. Despite the blood loss, she was conscious, if weak. He still had his arm around her back to support her in the water. As he headed them toward the boats, he didn't want to let her go.

Ever.

He'd been denying his feelings for her, but he couldn't any more.

"How are you doing?" he asked.

Though her voice was weak, she said, "I'll live."

"You'd better stay with me, Cordy."

"I don't have the strength to go anywhere myself."

"I don't mean just now."

He pulled her closer to his side, careful not to hurt her.

From the moment he'd met Cordelia, he couldn't see life without her by his side. She reminded him of someone he'd known once long ago, someone he couldn't quite place... almost as if he were trying to remember a different lifetime. He'd told himself that he was only after the treasure, had convinced himself she was simply another child of privilege to be dismissed, had tried to erase her from his mind and heart, had steeled himself from giving in to what he'd thought as lunacy.

But no matter the argument, his heart had its say. Cordelia was intelligent and strong and brave. And while he'd thought no one here gave a damn about him, she'd risked her own life to save his.

Emmett the seafaring poet had been right on the money when he'd said love might be the most valuable treasure of all.

By the time they reached the *Evening Star*, Madelyn was at the rail, peering down at them in the water with a concerned expression. "What's going on?"

"First," Cordelia said, her voice weak but steady. "I'm fine, no reason to worry."

Madelyn gasped. "Your trying to assure me makes me worry all the more!"

Morgan helped Cordelia up the ladder. The wound might have closed, but blood loss could be serious. She might need a transfusion.

When her mother saw the tear in Cordelia's swimsuit, she went pale. "Let me see." Madelyn pulled away the cut material and cried out at the crescent-shaped scar.

And though Morgan had been the one to seal the

wound, he still felt somewhat disbelieving at the magic that had saved her.

Madelyn grabbed her daughter to her and began to cry. "I could have lost you, too."

"It's okay, Mom. I'm fine. We're fine."

Madelyn looked around. "What about Innis?"

Cordelia opened her mouth as if to tell her mother about him, but in the end, she simply shook her head.

"She's in shock," Morgan said, wrapping an arm around Cordelia to hold her close.

"I don't understand." Madelyn's confusion was clear. "What happened?"

"Innis was trying to kill me, and Cordelia pushed him out of the way."

"Oh, my, oh…" Putting a hand to her mouth as the blood drained from her face, Madelyn looked as if she was in shock, as well.

"We're going in to get Cordelia checked out by a doctor." Picking her up in his arms, Morgan resisted crushing her to him lest he press against the seemingly healed wound.

He carried her to a padded deck lounger where she could rest. Her mother brought a light blanket and covered her. He looked over to the *Sea Rover*. Emmett was at the rail, looking concerned.

"We're going in!" Morgan shouted. "You stay out here. The divers don't go down until the after the authorities clear the site." He turned to Foley's divers, who were equally interested in what was going on. "You, too. Stay put."

"Where's Foley?" one of them called back.

"Shark bait."

A horrified expression crossed the man's face.

As Morgan took over the *Evening Star* on engine power rather than sail and headed the yacht in toward Crescent Key, he knew no one would go down to the wreck site before what was left of Innis Foley was retrieved.

Madelyn had fetched orange juice for Cordelia to drink to help stabilize her. Cordelia was catching her mother up on the details of what had happened to them, and Morgan realized Madelyn already knew things he didn't.

She said, "I told you if Elizabeth and Will were trying to find each other again, Carlyle would try to stop them."

Elizabeth...Will...Carlyle...

Familiar names, and according to his research, all connected with the mother lode on the *Celestine* when it sank four hundred years ago.

"You don't have to worry any longer, Mom. It's over now." Cordelia took her mother's hand, saying, "You look a little shaken. Maybe you should go lie down until we get to the dock."

"What about you?"

"I need the air. Don't worry, Morgan won't let anything happen to me." She inclined her head as if signaling her mother to leave them alone.

Madelyn nodded and left.

Cordelia looked as if she were trying to get to her feet.

"Stay right there!" Morgan ordered. Putting the boat on autopilot, he joined her. "You need to be resting, too." Though he would rather she did it here, where he could keep an eye on her.

"Probably. But oddly enough, I'm feeling a little better, and I want to talk to you."

"About?"

"How did you know to use the crescent to stop the bleeding?" she asked. "I read about Elizabeth using it trying to save Will in her journal, but how did you know?"

He said, "Instinct," because she wouldn't believe the truth.

"Liar. How?"

Morgan sighed. Considering the circumstances, perhaps the truth wouldn't sound so outlandish. "A voice told me what to do."

"A woman?"

He shook his head. "A man. He said the girdle was spun with magic and that the crescent would save you."

"Will," she whispered.

His ancestor. Was it possible?

"I didn't know what else to do, so I put my faith in what he told me." He hesitated a moment, then added, "It wasn't the first time."

"That you healed someone?"

"The voice, Cordy, the voice. How do you think I found you when you ran out of air? And before that. It all started after I found this ring. I kept seeing things…hearing things…but I convinced myself the expedition had simply kicked my imagination into high gear."

She took his hand and placed hers next to his so the rings lined up. She read, "Doubt the stars are fire…yet never doubt my love." She fell silent for a moment, then said, "About my siding with Innis…I'm so sorry I suspected you, Morgan. I had time to think everything over carefully and realized you weren't to blame. I knew you were in danger." She licked her lips. "I'd dreamed it more than once."

"Are you saying you're psychic?"

"Something like that."

Cordelia then told him about her precognitive dreams and the fact that she saw one man cut the other's air hose. She told him how she'd been determined to find and destroy the dagger before that could happen.

"What made you decide that I wasn't the killer?" he asked.

"I think it was the look in your eyes after I let Innis convince me you messed with my gauge. I couldn't get it out of my mind."

"I was angry."

"You were hurt. Among other things."

Morgan would have liked to deny it, but he couldn't. Not wanting to expose himself further to her, he gruffly said, "Get some rest now, Cordy. You need time to recuperate. We'll be at the marina in twenty minutes."

Cordelia gave him a long, lingering look that made his pulse race and made him wish for things between them that were never going to happen. Not that he looked away. He loved her with everything he was, and if she could only be honest, she would admit she felt the same for him.

His return gaze challenged her to be brave in all things, including matters of the heart.

Cordelia was feeling a little stronger by the time they pulled into the marina. Morgan had radioed ahead for the authorities. An ambulance was waiting to take her and Mom to the medical center. The rational part of her understood why Morgan stayed behind to make out an incident report and to lead the investigators to the wreck site. But the other part of her deep inside didn't want to let him out of her sight.

He was *her* Will…

At the medical center, she was poked and prodded by a doctor who marveled at the incredible way the cut had healed but told her she would live. He kept her overnight for observation, in addition to giving her a transfusion. He also said she would have to take it easy for several days. No diving for at least a week.

Which left the wreck site open to a pirate.

If Morgan really was one.

Cordelia didn't want to think it, not after all they'd been through. But he'd made no commitment to her. They'd formed no legal partnership, and Morgan didn't know it was their destiny to be together.

Cordelia waited for him to come to her. Waited while she went through tests. Waited while she was put in a bed where she was given fluids and a pint of blood. Frustrated at being kept to her bed for several hours even with Mom's company, once the transfusion was finished, she tried to get up.

"What are you doing?" her mother asked, moving quickly to prevent her feet from hitting the floor. "Stay put. I'll get whatever you need."

"I need to see Morgan."

"You'll stay right here," Mom insisted. "Do as the doctor ordered. You don't even know where Morgan is at the moment."

"Can you find out?"

"I'll call the marina. Surely someone there can tell me."

Cordelia lay back in bed as Mom made that call.

"Hello, I'm trying to reach Morgan Murphy." Mom paused. "Yes, I can wait." Another pause and then, "I see. Can you get a message to him when he returns? Please tell him that Cordelia Ward must spend the night at the medical center." She gave her cell number, then said, "Thank you so much." She met Cordelia's gaze. "He's still at the site with the authorities. Don't worry, he'll call."

Call? Surely he would come for her if only to make sure she was all right for himself.

Her mother sat by her side, keeping her company and telling stories about Cordelia's father that happened before she'd been born. Cordelia listened, her mother's voice soothing her. Morgan's face the last thing she saw before falling asleep.

After leaving the dive site, Morgan headed for the marina where he boarded *Foley's Treasure* to face down the cook. Certain she'd put the gris-gris on him, he would find out for himself if she'd had a part in this tragedy. But according to the crew, Brigitte and her husband Leandre were nowhere to be found. They'd vanished within minutes of docking.

He called the hospital as soon as he got the message from Cordelia's mother, even though it was late. He was disappointed when Madelyn Ward answered rather than Cordelia.

"I was tied up with the authorities until a little while ago. Cordy is all right, isn't she? Can I speak to her?"

"She's fine. She's sleeping now. I don't want to wake her."

Sleep was probably the best prescription for her after all

she'd been through fighting Innis, so Morgan didn't argue.

"What did the doctor say about her wound?"

"That it's spontaneous healing was quite unusual," Madelyn said, voice ripe with questions she didn't ask. "He ordered a transfusion and fluids and such. He wanted to keep her overnight as a precaution."

"Good. I'm surprised she didn't insist on leaving."

"She did, actually."

Morgan had to smile at that. He could imagine her giving the doctors and her mother a hard time. "You're sure she's all right?"

"She was weak and needed rest, but yes, I think so. I'm staying in her room to make certain she stays that way. What about you?"

"I wasn't the one hurt, Madelyn."

"Not physically, perhaps, but you've been through something unbelievable."

He really had. He was still trying to come to terms with it all himself. "I'm good. Call me tomorrow when the doctors sign off on Cordy, would you? Then I'll meet you at the marina."

"All right."

Having returned to the *Evening Star*, Morgan lay back in Cordelia's bunk after moving the book sitting on the mattress. Though he was exhausted, he was worrying about her despite her mother's reassurances. Part of him wanted to rush to the medical center to see for himself, but she needed that sleep more than she needed him.

If only he could sleep…

Glancing over to the shelf where he'd put the book, he realized it looked like a very old journal. He picked it up and held it for a moment, instinct urging him to open it and check out the contents. The pages were fragile, as was the ink put to parchment. And he noted the date of the first entry—1601.

A chill ran through him as he began to read:

> *Dunham Castle, 1601*
>
> *ON THIS DAY I shall begin a journey inevitable from the moment I was born on Midsummer Eve, Witches' Night. My nursemaid proclaimed that I am marked as a child of magic.*
>
> *Yet I am not a witch, for the face of my beloved and what awaits me at journey's end is shrouded from me by the veil of time. I know only that with him I shall scale peaks higher than my spirit could ever strive to reach alone, and because of him, I shall descend into valleys which will try my soul...*

As he continued reading entry after entry, the past opened up to him in a way that no sunken treasure could ever reveal. He lost himself in Elizabeth and Will's story, reading until the first streaks of dawn signaled a new day.

And when he finished the last page, he understood.

Cordelia awoke to daybreak to find her mother asleep in the chair next to her bed.

Morgan hadn't come to see her. The knowledge choked her.

What was going on? Was he back working the site?

Unable to stay in the bed for another hour, Cordelia

rose and took a quick shower and dressed. Miraculously, she felt fine, as if nothing had ever happened to her.

Too bad the crescent couldn't have saved Will for Elizabeth.

When she left the bathroom, her mother was awake. "I want to get out of here. Now."

"You have to wait a little while longer until you're cleared, Cordelia. A nurse just poked her head in the door and said the doctor was making his rounds. He'll be here in a few minutes. Sit."

Cordelia was too nervous to sit. She walked to the window and looked out into a garden area. "I want to know what is going on. I can't believe Morgan didn't come."

"He called to check on you after you fell asleep."

"Did he leave a message?"

"Yes, he asked me to call him back once you were medically cleared and that he would meet us at the marina."

Nothing more personal?

Deflated, Cordelia sank into silence as she waited for the doctor to arrive. Those few minutes turned into more than an hour. Then she had to wait for paperwork. And had to be transported out in a wheelchair to a waiting taxi.

Once in the cab, her mother said, "Morgan asked me to call to let him know when we were on our way. Would you rather call him yourself?"

Not knowing what she was about to face, Cordelia found her internal strength. "Let's surprise him."

It was midmorning by the time they arrived at the marina.

No surprise to find Morgan the center of a growing crowd and a television news team.

Cordelia couldn't breathe for a moment—couldn't step out of the vehicle—when she expected Morgan had already claimed the mother lode and had edged her out of the find. Certainly a reason for the media being there.

She looked to Morgan, who didn't move, simply stood silently, eyes hidden behind sunglasses, hands shoved into his pockets, shoulders hunched, hair whipping around his beard-stubbled face.

Even with the car protecting her, she wasn't free of his influence. A live wire seemed to connect them, to pulse through her, from her ring to him to her heart. He wasn't responding to her in any visible way, but his emotions filled her.

Morgan wouldn't betray her any more than Will would have betrayed Elizabeth.

She took a deep breath and gave him her trust

As she exited the taxi, the cameras turned on her.

"Ms. Ward," a reporter said, "I understand you found the *Celestine's* mother lode."

Her pulse fluttering with a happiness she could hardly contain, Cordelia looked to Morgan, who didn't say a word. Obviously he'd told them she was responsible. And as tempting as it might be to take the credit as he apparently intended, she wasn't about to. She might have been the one to find the wreck, but he had found Elizabeth's girdle.

"You understand wrong," she told the reporter. "Mr. Murphy is the one who found the mother lode."

"Murphy, tell us about it," a woman said.

Morgan gave the pretty reporter his best media smile. "Ms. Ward is being too generous. The person really responsible for the recovery of the *Celestine* and its mother lode is her father, the late Dr. Clive Ward. His years of careful research and his meticulous mapping pointed the way." He aimed his smile straight at Cordelia. "He deserves every bit of credit. We merely carried out his legacy."

Cordelia's heart soared and her ring sent out tingles that made her certain...

...*the wait was over.*

"So you're partners in this?" another reporter asked.

Morgan gave Cordelia a look that seared her down to her toes and said, "I can't think of anyone I would rather partner with."

"Nor I." Cordelia moved to his side.

"What will the two of you do with all that treasure?"

Morgan put his arm around her waist and Cordelia leaned into his warmth and strength and thought she could stay there forever.

He said, "The treasure belongs in a fine museum."

She added, "With my mother, Dr. Madelyn Ward, as curator."

Still standing at the taxi that had brought them here, Mom gave her a radiant smile, and Cordelia knew she'd been right—the promise of challenging work was exactly what her mother needed.

Finally, Morgan took her in his arms. Her birthmark thrummed and her ring sent a sweet longing up her arm and down to her center. And when Morgan's mouth covered hers, Cordelia knew their love had been destined.

Epilogue

Dressed in a long-sleeved, ankle-length, diaphanous white gown that showed off her cleavage and nearly every inch of her long legs, Cordelia picked up Elizabeth's celestial girdle. Morgan had recovered it from where it had returned to its sandy grave. Searchers had found no sign of Innis or of the shark attack. If she didn't have the crescent scar to assure her, she might think they'd imagined it all.

The girdle gave off a sense of wonderment and hope, traits that she'd admired in Elizabeth, and because of her strong connection with her ancestress, her idea that she and Elizabeth were somehow one, Cordelia secured the girdle around her waist.

She stared at her image in the full-length mirror.

Who would Morgan see?

He'd given her a half hour to ready herself—said he could only be apart from her for so long—and only half that had passed. She sat at the dressing table and pulled her long, blond hair up in a twist and secured it with a clip set with a sapphire-studded star and ruby crescent moon.

And then she opened the top of the treasure box and lovingly touched the journal of the woman who had first worn the Posey ring. Elizabeth had been a woman bound to duty with few choices in her life. Cordelia's life had been filled with choices. She'd been able to be anyone, do anything she wanted. Getting to this privileged life had been a painful process that had taken centuries.

Cordelia understood Elizabeth's charge now. Elizabeth had used her journal to speak directly to her. Cordelia had been privy to her mind and magic.

To the journal she would store in the box, Cordelia would add the chain and crescent that connected her back to Elizabeth.

But not just yet.

For now, the chain remained around her neck, and the crescent dangled between her breasts. She hadn't removed it since Morgan had used it to save her life.

Opening Elizabeth's journal to the first blank page, she began to write.

Murphy's Point, Moonspinner Key, 2013

I am in Morgan's home now and never have been happier.

I owe it to you, Elizabeth, for your never-ending love story captivated me from the first page.

I feel one with you and I wonder if you somehow feel it, too. Did you help to save our lives when Innis would see us dead, or did I hear your whispers simply to appease my own heart?

Together, Morgan and I have at last conquered that which has shadowed our lives. I am confident the evil is banished, for, together, Morgan and I ended the curse on the rings that connect us forever to you and Will.

I have recovered fully and in the moon that has passed, have found joy working side by side with Morgan to raise the Celestine's mother lode, an auspicious beginning to our life together.

Tonight will take us a step closer. We chose to start over, to get to know each other as only two people whose souls are joined can do. But tonight, we will join our bodies as you did with Will. Following your example, I plan to record Morgan's and my journey together from this day forward, so that my daughter and the women who follow her may know us and the paths we take.

I hear the clock strike ten.

It is time.

My new husband awaits.

Filled with anticipation, Cordelia closed the journal, rose and turned to find Morgan waiting for her in the open patio doorway. He was dressed in tight, knee-length black pants and an open, full-sleeved white shirt that billowed in the breeze, revealing a body chiseled by the gods. His dark hair whipped around his rugged face to reveal the emerald in his right ear. As he had the first time they'd met, he looked every bit the dangerous pirate.

Her lips quivered, and she couldn't hold back her grin.

A smile that equaled hers softened his fierce expression, and he held out his hand for her to join him. Together, they set out into the near dark, crossing the patio to the sandy path leading to the water's edge.

As always, she was drawn to the night sky so like the one a month ago when their magical adventure began.

There was something special about this sky.

About this moon.

These stars.

This night.

"The same moon under which I discovered the Posey ring," he said.

"And I Elizabeth's journal."

With the water lapping over their bare feet, Morgan swept her into his arms and kissed her breathless. She was ready for him, had been ready for what felt like four centuries.

He wrapped his hands around the girdle and pulled her against him, and she could feel the strength of his desire through her filmy gown. Her pulse raced and her heart thundered when he lowered his head to her breasts. Her eyes fluttered closed as his lips found the valley between them.

Light, sensual kisses traveled downward, valley to belly, belly to juncture. He spread her gown. She spread her thighs. Already wet for him, she threw back her head and gasped with pleasure when he drank her in.

She'd been waiting her whole life for this.

She wanted to be one with him through this and every lifetime.

The pressure in her quickly mounted and spread, and she tore at his hair to that he would stop before she came.

"Together," she whispered.

"Always."

He stripped out of the knee pants and tossed them on the sand. The waning moon loved his turgid flesh. He was hard and beautiful and he was hers.

He kissed her again and swayed, bringing her with him, so they fell together in the shallows. The tide coming in washed over them. She in her gown and Elizabeth's girdle, he in his full-sleeved shirt, they rolled and laughed and got soaking wet, and when they finally stopped, she landed on top.

Heart pounding, she stared at his face as she mounted him, so wet that he slid inside, sleek and deep. He ran his hands up her thighs, one thumb lingering at her heart, the other hand cupping a breast and thumbing a nipple through the material. Never taking her gaze from his beloved face, she spread her hands over his naked chest and began the rhythm that would lift them to the stars.

As they pleasured each other, her mind filled with the love story that had sealed her fate with this man. Words tumbled through her head, their magic pulling her back in time.

The part of me which never dies will find Will at last. If I combed the earth and searched through the stars, there is no being I would want but this one. Again passion shall beat between us like a living force.

I long for this with every breath I draw.

"Will...?" Cordelia whispered.

"...is it truly you?" Elizabeth finished.

His fingertips brushed her throat and her skin heated under his touch.

"I have returned to you. How can I take away any doubt, love?"

The growing pressure within her body made her voice husky. "Perhaps memories..."

He stroked her hair, lifting it in a mass to his face. "I can still smell its lavender scent when we walked to the pond behind my grandfather's cottage. I followed you to paradise there, love. The water gave life to our daughter."

Her senses battered by hope and fear, she mused, "Is that why we both love the sea so much now?"

With a murmured agreement, his mouth rocked gently over her parted lips.

She abandoned herself to his touch, his hands caressing her breasts, her thighs, all of her.

"Oh, Will." She murmured his name over and over as her burning desire heightened.

"Remember, love, our last day in the glade?"

Soul-deep sadness ravaged her body and she buried her face in his shoulder. "No! No, never that memory."

He cupped her face and she gazed into his beloved blue eyes. They were rich with luster and lit by flames of life brighter than she had ever seen.

"No one knows what happened there except us. Remember what you said to me, Elizabeth? You must."

Shudders rocked her body. "I promised I would overcome Carlyle's curse. That this was not the end for us. I knew I carried your child, and I promised Stephen would be granted his birthright." Tears blinded her, making Will's face shimmer with an unearthly beauty. "Our Serena ruled beside Stephen. They were great and just. As you would have been."

His smile urged her on.

"Then I said, for us heaven can wait. If it takes a thousand lifetimes, we will be together again."

He curved their bodies closer, his face hovering above hers. "And I said, I believe you, Elizabeth." Slowly, he brushed her lips again and again. "Love, you have kept all your promises," he whispered thickly. "Now it is time for me to keep my promise given to you in my old bedroom at my grandfather's cottage."

Their gazes melted together, a slow unlocking of all they had been and the hope of what would be.

He murmured, "I promise we shall have nights like this through eternity. This time, I am yours forever."

At last under his adoring hands and gazing into his eyes, she reached the heaven he offered her. Her heart couldn't be fuller.

"I believe you, Will."

She rolled, taking him with her so that he was now on top.

"I'm yours forever, Cordy."

"I believe you, Morgan, and I'm yours."

Their love had been written in the stars.

Though they'd had to wait four centuries to find heaven together, their time was now.

About the Authors

SHERRILL BODINE is an author, fashionista, and world traveler. She helped develop and co-wrote a comic book, published nineteen romance novels, including *Talk of the Town* which was a Red Hot Read from *Cosmopolitan* Magazine and *A Black Tie Affair* which was a Fresh Fiction Fresh Pick. She is frequently featured in Michigan Avenue Magazine and was a contributing columnist to the *Chicago Sun-Times*. She currently resides in Chicago where she attends fashion shows and charity galas with her longtime Prince Charming when she's not pursuing her passion for family, films, books and travel.

New York Times and *USA Today* bestselling author PATRICIA ROSEMOOR has had 96 novels published with more than 7 million books in print. Patricia writes romantic suspense or paranormal romantic thrillers. She also writes a less pulse-pounding combination of romance and suspense with a dash of humor with a partner as Lynn Patrick. Patricia has won a Golden Heart from Romance Writers of America and two Reviewers Choice and two Career Achievement Awards from Romantic Times Book Reviews.